The spider was moving again . . .

Mikey couldn't react quickly enough. The glass with the spider inside slid to the edge of the table and went crashing to the floor.

"Watch out!" Max shrieked, jumping up onto one of the chairs in a panic.

Mikey did the same thing. He was sure that the spider was now running around on the floor. And he was terrified that it was going to run right up his pant leg.

But Mikey was wrong. The spider wasn't on the floor at all. It was clinging to the edge of the table, baring two razor-sharp fangs . . .

D0831636

DEADTIME STORIES™
Along Came a Spider

A. G. Cascone

Troll

*For Larry, Moe, and Curley
a.k.a.
Roger, Chuckie,
and last but never least,
Mike*

Published by Troll Communications L.L.C.

Deadtime Stories is a trademark of Annette Cascone and Gina Cascone.

Printed in the United States of America.

10 9 8 7 6 5 4 3 2 1

CHAPTER 1

Mikey Davis froze as a thousand hairy legs crept across the carpet. *Oh, man,* Mikey thought, watching the horrid little beast slither its way toward his best friend, Max. *That creepy, crawly creature is about to attack!*

Before Mikey could even make a sound, the hairy-looking creature did just that.

Mikey bolted up like a shot.

But Max Edwards didn't move. He just lay there, flat on his back, as the thing climbed up his collar and slithered into his ear.

Mikey couldn't bear to watch. "Ewwwwwww, geeeezz!" he cried, covering his eyes. He was sure that the creepy crawler was going to eat its way through Max's brain and wiggle out his other ear!

"What's the matter with you?" Max finally reacted.

"You've got a thousand-legger digging in your ear," Mikey hollered at him.

"Do not!" Max protested, slapping away at his ears.

Mikey ducked as the fat, juicy millipede flew out of Max's ear and hit the wall behind Mikey.

"Oh, gross!" Max sprang up in a panic. He stared at the disgusting bug as it ran across the wall. "Why didn't you tell me that thing was crawling on me?" he complained, digging his fingers into both ears.

"I didn't have a chance before he jumped right into your ear," Mikey said. "Didn't you feel him squiggling around in there?"

"No," Max shot back, digging even deeper into his ears. The stuff he pulled out and wiped on his jeans was almost as disgusting as the millipede.

"Aw, geez." Mikey cringed. "No wonder you didn't feel him. You've got a potato farm growing in there!"

"Shut up," Max grumbled. "At least I don't have bugs in my room!"

"Well, I didn't have any bugs in here either until you opened your suitcase," Mikey shot back. "It's *your* bug," he insisted. "Now get rid of it."

"No way," Max said, shaking his head. "I'm not touching that thing. You get rid of it."

"I'm not touching it either," Mikey said.

Just then Fluffy poked her fat little face into Mikey's room and meowed.

Max's eyes lit up. "Make that froufrou cat get the bug," he suggested.

"Fluffy?" Mikey rolled his eyes. "Forget about it. That cat's a total loser. She doesn't even have claws."

Fluffy the froufrou cat belonged to Alison, Mikey's thirteen-year-old froufrou sister. Mikey hated them both. Fluffy was every bit as snotty as Alison. But at least the cat couldn't talk back. Whenever Alison opened her mouth, Mikey wanted to deck her.

Alison thought she was the coolest thing on earth because she was *already* a teenager, and Mikey still had a year and a half to go. She constantly called him a "baby" or a "jerk."

"Get out of here," Mikey screamed at the cat. But the cat just stood there, ignoring him.

"Scram," Mikey shouted at the annoying fur ball again. He looked around for something to throw at her.

"Wait. Don't chase her away." Max's eyes lit up. He moved toward Fluffy slowly, until he was close enough to scoop her up into his arms. "Let's see if we can get her to eat the bug."

"That's disgusting," Mikey said. But he laughed. He loved the idea of making Fluffy eat a big, fat, juicy bug. Alison would go crazy when she found out. And Mikey couldn't wait to tell her. He only hoped that a whole bunch of hairy little bug legs would get stuck in Fluffy's whiskers when she chowed down on the thing. Then Mikey would have proof.

But Fluffy wouldn't even look at the bug, much less eat it.

"This cat really *is* a loser," Max griped. He was holding

Fluffy so that her face was only an inch away from the bug on the wall. But Fluffy just hung there in his hands, limp as a rag doll.

Meanwhile the millipede ran down the wall, across the floorboard, and back onto the carpet.

"Get it, you stupid cat!" Max tossed Fluffy onto the floor. She landed right on top of the bug. But all she did was lie down.

The millipede dashed across the carpet and disappeared under Mikey's bed.

"Now look what you've done," Mikey hollered at Max. "You made the stupid thing run under my bed."

"So?" Max shot back.

"Sooooo," Mikey huffed. "There's no way I'm going to be able to sleep in that bed knowing that bug is under there. What if it climbs into bed with me while I'm sleeping and crawls into *my* ear?" The thought was way too gross.

Max rolled his eyes.

"I'm serious," Mikey said. "And if you don't help me catch him, I swear I'll find him and stick him up your nose this time."

Mikey got down on his hands and knees to look under his bed. Max hit the floor beside him.

"I don't see him anywhere," Mikey said.

"That's because you've got too much junk under here," Max pointed out. "You're never going to find that bug."

Mikey wasn't about to give up. He started pulling things out from under his bed, looking for the millipede.

There was dirty laundry, empty cereal bowls, old sneakers, loose change, pieces from games he'd thrown out long ago, but no bug.

"Help me out here," he said to Max, who was just lying there doing nothing.

The minute Max reached under the bed, he started to scream. "Something's got me!" he shouted, pulling his hand away fast.

Mikey laughed when he saw what was attached to Max's fingers. "That's just duct tape, you idiot."

"Oh, yeah?" Max shot back, peeling the roll of tape off his hand. "Then how come it's sticky on the wrong side?"

"It's sticky on both sides," Mikey told him. "It's two-sided tape. Pretty cool, huh?"

"I guess," Max said, tossing the roll aside as Mikey continued digging under the bed.

"I think I see him," Mikey told Max. "Over there," he said, pointing, "on top of that box."

"That's him all right," Max agreed.

Mikey eased the box out from under the bed.

The millipede stood frozen on the lid.

"Squash him," Mikey told Max.

Just then the bug started running.

Instead of trying to squash the thing, Max did something else. He blew on it.

"What are you doing?" Mikey asked.

"Blowing on him," Max answered. "If you blow on bugs, they stay perfectly still. It must scare them or something."

Max was right. When he blew on the bug it stood still. But

while he was explaining that to Mikey, it took off again.

"Get him!" Mikey cried as the millipede raced across the lid.

"I'll blow on him," Max said. "You squash him."

Max started to blow not a moment too soon. The bug was already at the edge of the box, about to escape.

Mikey looked around for something that he could use to squash the bug, while Max's breath kept it still. Finally, he spotted the perfect thing—the roll of two-sided tape.

Mikey grabbed the tape and raised it up over the bug.

But Max ran out of breath. As Mikey smashed the roll of tape down onto the box, the millipede skittered over the edge and disappeared under the lid.

"Darn it!" Mikey hollered. "I can't believe you let him get away again, Max."

"It wasn't my fault," Max defended himself. "You moved too slow. Besides, he didn't get away—he went inside the box."

"Open the lid," Mikey ordered. "I'll get him."

"No way," Max shot back. "This time *I'll* smash him. You blow."

But Mikey didn't get the chance to open the box, because when Max grabbed for the roll of tape, the lid came up with it.

"Blow!" Max instructed as he struggled to free the tape from the lid of the box.

But Mikey was too horrified to even think about trying to blow. Because what he saw inside the box was a lot more gruesome than one little bug.

CHAPTER

2

Every inch of Mikey's skin suddenly felt as if it were crawling. Quickly he turned away from the horrible sight. He'd forgotten all about the slimy dead bodies under his bed. And he couldn't stand to watch Max pulling them out of their box.

"Way cool!" Max exclaimed, examining each and every specimen.

"That stuff is gross," Mikey said, feeling his stomach lurch. "Just put it away."

"Why didn't you tell me you had a dissecting kit?" Max rubbed his hands together like some kind of mad scientist.

"I forgot I had it," Mikey answered. It had been under his bed, untouched, for nearly two years. It was the worst birthday present Mikey had ever gotten. But his mother wouldn't let him throw it in the garbage because it was from his cousin, Ernest.

Ernest had insisted that his gift was the best, because it was "educational *and* fun" all at the same time. But Mikey couldn't believe that Ernest had given him a bunch of dead bugs for his birthday, especially since bugs were just about Mikey's least favorite thing on earth. He'd even thrown up his birthday cake after opening the box.

"Check this out," Max said. He shoved one of the jars from the kit in Mikey's face.

"Get that away from me!" Mikey yelled, pushing Max.

The jar was full of clear liquid, with a dead, shriveled frog floating in it.

"Come on," Max said eagerly. "Let's play with this."

Max pulled the other jars out of the box. Besides the frog, there was a fat, juicy worm, a beetle, a cricket, a cockroach, and a big, black, hairy spider, each floating in its own jar of liquid.

There was also a microscope and a box of dissecting tools.

Mikey didn't want anything to do with any of it.

"Don't take all that stuff out of the box," he said to Max.

"Why?" Max asked as he kept right on doing it. "This will be fun."

"What about Ice Land?" Mikey asked. "My mom will be back any minute to take us." Mikey knew it was probably not true. His mom was at the mall shopping with Alison for a new outfit for Alison to wear to one of her froufrou friend's parties. And while Mikey's mom had promised to drive Mikey and Max to Ice Land when she got back, Mikey was sure that the skating rink would be closed long before Alison picked out an outfit. But Mikey would say anything to avoid having to dissect a bunch of disgusting stuff.

"Your mom's never coming back," Max complained. "And it's not like we have anything else to do. Not around here anyway," he added. "Next time, you should spend the weekend at my house."

Max was right. There was nothing for the two of them to do in Mikey's neighborhood—because Mikey and his family didn't live in a neighborhood. They lived out in the "boondocks"—at least that's what Alison called it. There was nothing around for miles but farmland and woods. Their closest neighbor was a good ten-minute drive away.

"Come on," Max continued to plead. "I didn't come here so we could sit around your room doing nothing. At least now we have something cool to do."

There was no way out of it. Max was determined to play with the dissecting kit. But Mikey wasn't about to let him do it in his bedroom.

"Let's take it down into the kitchen," Mikey suggested. "We'll have lots more room. And the sink is right there in case we get anything gross on ourselves."

"Good idea," Max agreed. He quickly tossed everything back into the box and headed for the door.

"Have you ever seen frog guts?" Max asked as the two of them tromped down the steps.

"No," Mikey answered. "And I really don't want to either."

But Max did. He hurried into the kitchen and started setting everything up on the table.

Mikey just stood in the doorway watching him.

"Why don't you get us some soda and chips to snack on while we do this?" Max suggested. "Make yourself useful."

"You're disgusting," Mikey told Max. "How can you possibly eat while you're cutting out guts?"

Max grinned. "Watch me," he said.

Mikey got the snacks while Max continued to set up his little operating room. When Mikey finally sat down at the table, Max was ready to go.

"Let's do the frog first," Max said with a smile.

"Don't you think you should start with something small?" Mikey suggested. "Like maybe the worm. Just so you can get the hang of it."

"You know what I think?" Max sneered. "I think you're chicken."

Max was right. But there was no way in the world that Mikey was going to admit it. "Am not," he said.

"Then let's do the frog."

"Fine," Mikey huffed.

It didn't really matter whether or not Mikey agreed. Max was already opening the jar with the frog inside it. When he got the lid off, he reached into the jar with his bare fingers and pulled out the frog.

Mikey cringed.

"Too cool," Max said as he examined the green, shriveled body. Then he dangled it in front of Mikey's face, just to gross him out.

It worked. But being grossed out was nothing compared to what happened next.

As Max slapped the frog down onto the dissecting tray, Mikey saw it twitch.

"Uh, Max," Mikey began. "Did you—"

But before Mikey could finish, something even more shocking happened. The frog jumped!

CHAPTER 3

"It's alive!" Mikey shrieked in horror. "That frog is alive!" Mikey pushed himself away from the table so fast, his chair toppled over backward.

Max cracked up.

"It's not funny!" Mikey insisted, pulling himself up. "That frog just jumped!"

Max kept on laughing.

"I'm telling you," Mikey huffed, "it's alive!"

Only now it didn't look alive. The frog was lying on the tray, looking as dead as it had looked in the jar.

Mikey leaned over to see if the frog was breathing. But its shriveled, green body wasn't moving—until Mikey's nose was a couple of inches away from it.

"Ri-bit!"

Mikey jumped back again as the frog let out a loud

croak and leaped from the dissecting tray.

"Oooooooooooh, grooooooooossssssss!" Mikey screamed.

"Ri-bit!" Max belched another croak, waving the frog in front of Mikey's face.

"You're such a jerk!" Mikey hollered, pushing Max's hand away. "I can't believe you did that!"

"And you're an idiot." Max laughed, dropping the frog back onto the tray. "Look, Mikey." Max plinked the frog into the air with his finger. "It's alive! He's jumping again!"

"Very funny," Mikey said.

"You're such a weenie," Max taunted.

"I am not," Mikey insisted.

"Oh, yeah?" Max said. "Then how come you're afraid to touch him?"

"I'm not," Mikey lied.

"Then prove it," Max dared.

"There," Mikey said, touching the side of the slimy, wet body with the tip of his finger. "Are you happy now?"

"Any weenie could do that," Max informed him.

"What do you want me to do? Hug him?" Mikey snapped.

But Max suggested something much worse. "Pin him to the dissecting board so we can operate."

"You pin him," Mikey told Max, cringing at the thought. "You're the one who wants to cut him up."

"See," Max teased. "You *are* a weenie."

Max picked up the frog and spread him out on the board, like the picture in the instruction booklet. But when Max reached for the first pin, Mikey grabbed it away from him.

"Give me that thing," Mikey said. "I'll do it." Pushing a couple of pins through a dead frog was a whole lot easier than listening to Max call him a "weenie" for the rest of his life.

"You've got to push them right through his little bones," Max told him, smirking.

Mikey winced as he pushed the first pin through the frog's front foot. He thought he was going to throw up. Especially when Max reached for a potato chip and started munching away.

"Now you've got to nail his back feet down," Max said.

"I know," Mikey shot back. He was grossed out enough as it was. He didn't need to hear Max's play-by-play instructions. "There," he said, pushing the last pin through. "He's all yours."

"Aren't you gonna carve him up with me?" Max asked. "It'll be good practice. We'll have to do this in school next year, you know."

"No, thanks," Mikey said. "I don't want to practice." He didn't want to watch either. Especially when Max started sawing away.

"These tools stink," Max said, struggling to cut through the frog's chest with the little scalpel that came with the kit. "Give me a steak knife or something."

"No way!" Mikey refused. "My mother will kill me if she finds out we were carving out frog guts with her steak knives."

"Well, there's no way I can cut through him with this thing," Max shot back. "Even safety scissors are sharper."

"Tough," Mikey said. "Push harder."

Max did just that.

A minute later Mikey was sorry he'd suggested it—frog guts went flying everywhere.

"Ew, gross!" Mikey shrieked as a blue squiggly thing with two slimy red blobs dangling off the end landed in the center of the table. "What the heck is that?"

"I don't know," Max answered, still sawing away. "Maybe it's his kidneys. Look at the diagram."

"You're the one who wants to play surgeon," Mikey said. "*You* look at the diagram."

But Max didn't look at the diagram. He just kept pulling out frog guts.

"I hope you're not planning on being a doctor when you grow up," Mikey told Max. "You're supposed to know what you're operating on before you start cutting things out."

"You're right," Max said, working his way up to the frog's head. "I ought to do some brain surgery. At least I know where that is."

"Yeah," Mikey shot back. "And I bet his brain is a lot bigger than yours."

Max laughed as he kept cutting away. Mikey couldn't look. Luckily, it didn't take too long.

"This guy's done," Max said, scraping the frog brains off his scalpel. "Who's next?"

Mikey didn't even have a chance to answer before

Max dumped the worm out of the jar and sawed it in two.

"Why don't we do something else," Mikey finally suggested.

"Oh, come on," Max said. "Let's cut up one of the bugs."

"Bugs are no fun." Mikey tried to talk him out of it. "They don't have any guts."

"They must have some guts," Max disagreed. "Why else would they put them in a dissecting kit?"

"I guess so you can look at them under the microscope," Mikey said. "I mean, look at these guys." Mikey pointed to the beetle to make his point. "They're all crunchy. There's no way they've got any good guts."

For a second, it looked like Max was going to give in. Until he picked up the jar with the spider.

"Whoa," Max said. "I bet *he* has guts. Look at how fat he is."

Mikey rolled his eyes. Max wasn't about to quit.

"I've never seen a spider like this," Max continued. "He's huge!"

Not only was the spider huge, it was the ugliest thing Mikey had ever seen. It was black and hairy, with legs as long as a daddy longlegs, only thicker. Every inch of its fuzzy, fat body was covered with tiny red speckles. But most disgusting of all were the eight bulging black eyes that wrapped halfway around its entire body.

"What kind of spider is this?" Mikey asked Max.

"I don't know," Max said, reaching for the instruction

booklet. "Maybe it tells you in here."

Max flipped through the booklet until he landed on a page with a picture of the spider. "Too cool," he said, scanning the page. "It's called an a-rack-knee-a-bla-di-pha—" Max struggled for a second to pronounce the word. Then finally he just gave up. "It's a-rack-knee-a-something or other," he said in frustration. "And it's a killer!"

"It's poisonous?" Mikey asked.

"I don't know," Max answered, still skimming the booklet. "A-rack-knee-a-whatever-it-is 'comes from the deepest, darkest regions of South America,'" he read aloud. "'It is found only in the rain forests and is more dangerous than any other breed of a-rack-knees. A cross between the giant tarantula and the venomous black widow, this spider is far more deadly than either variety.'"

"Why?" Mikey asked.

Max turned to look at him. "Because it's a man-eater," he stated.

"What?" Mikey shrieked. "Let me see that thing." He grabbed the booklet from Max and scanned the page for himself. "It does not say that it's a 'man-eater,'" he informed Max. "It says it 'eats flesh.'"

"Same thing," Max insisted. He reached for the lid of the spider's jar and began to unscrew it.

"What are you doing?" Mikey asked nervously.

"I want to look at him," Max answered.

"Just leave him in the jar," Mikey told him.

"Calm down, you little weenie," Max snapped. "He's not gonna eat us. He's dead—remember?"

Mikey rolled his eyes. "Just don't cut him up, okay? In case he really is full of poisonous stuff or something."

"Oh, brother," Max sighed, dumping the spider onto the tray. "Give me the tweezers."

"Why?" Mikey asked. "What are you going to do?"

"I want to put him under the microscope so we can see him better," he told Mikey.

"Why don't you just pick him up with your fingers?" Mikey teased. "Are you chicken or something?"

"Just give me the tweezers," Max huffed.

"Here you go, you little *weenie*!" Mikey laughed as he handed them over.

The second Max began to pinch the tweezers closed around one of the spider's long, hairy legs, it started to move.

Only this time, Max wasn't playing a joke, because he started to scream.

A-rack-knee-a-whatever-it-was was moving all by itself—toward the closest piece of flesh it could find!

CHAPTER 4

"Holy smokes!" Max shrieked. He jumped from his chair as if there was a rocket under him. "That man-eating spider wants my finger! Get him back in the jar! Quick!"

The spider's eight bulging eyes rolled toward Mikey.

"You get him back in the jar!" Mikey screamed back. "There's no way I'm touching a killer spider that was supposed to be dead!"

"He's not a killer spider!" Max argued.

"Is too," Mikey insisted. "You said so yourself. That hairy little sucker is a man-eater!"

"He's too little to be a man-eater!" Max shouted. "Besides, the book didn't say that, remember? It said he eats flesh!"

"Well, every one of my fingers is covered with flesh,"

Mikey cried. "And I don't want that a-rack-kneed-whatever-it-is to bite any of it off!"

The spider skittered across the kitchen table toward Max.

"Do something!" Max yelled. "Before he really does try to eat me!"

With all the courage Mikey could muster, he quickly grabbed the jar from the edge of the table. But the lid was sitting right next to the dissecting tray, less than an inch away from the spider.

"Get the lid so we can scoop him back into the jar," Mikey told Max.

"No way I'm sticking my hand out near that spider," Max said.

"We need the lid!" Mikey's voice rose with his panic.

"Then get it!" Max yelled.

"Fine!" Mikey shouted. "Be a weenie!"

Mikey started to reach out slowly. He was careful to keep his arm high above the table as he moved for the lid.

The spider's eyes followed every move Mikey made. The second Mikey's hand was over the lid, the spider started for it.

Mikey's heart pounded. The spider looked ready to leap into the air and bite off all his fingers.

"Get it!" Max ordered.

Mikey wanted to, but he didn't know how.

If he moved too fast, he might startle the spider, and then it would really attack. But if he moved too slowly, the hairy little beast would have plenty of time to chomp down on his fingers.

Mikey wiggled his fingers in the air to see whether or not the spider would make a move.

It did. Only it wasn't the move Mikey expected.

Mikey pulled his arm away from the table so fast, he smacked Max hard in the face.

"Ooooch!" Max cried. "You just broke my nose!"

"Sorry," Mikey shot back. "I thought I was about to have my fingers bitten off!"

Instead of attacking Mikey's fingers, the spider had lunged for the lid of the jar. In fact, it had climbed on top of the thing, as if it were planning to guard it.

"Uh-oh," Max said. "Looks like somebody doesn't want to go back in the j-a-r."

Mikey rolled his eyes. "You don't have to spell it, you moron. That spider doesn't understand what you're saying."

"How do you know?" Max said. "He understands enough to know that we're trying to get him back in his, uh, home."

Max had a point. Mikey looked back at the eight-legged creature. "There's no way I'm grabbing that lid out from under him," he mumbled.

"Just smush him or something," Max suggested.

The second the words were out of Max's mouth, the spider took off across the table—as if it really did understand what Max was saying.

"Get him!" Mikey cried. "Before he gets away!"

"With what?" Max asked.

Mikey had an idea. "Blow on him," he told Max. "It worked with the millipede."

"I'm not putting my face near that sucker," Max shot back.

"Just do it!" Mikey ordered.

As Mikey reached for his soda, Max filled his lungs with enough air to blow down the three little pigs' houses.

"Blow!" Mikey yelled. Then he downed the last bit of soda in his glass.

Max blew. The spider stopped dead in its tracks.

As fast as he could, Mikey turned over his soda glass and plunked it down over the spider.

"Way to go!" Max exclaimed. "We got him!"

The spider pressed its bulging eyes against the walls of its prison and glared out at them.

"Uh-oh," Max said. "He looks pretty mad."

"Yeah," Mikey agreed. "If he gets out of this glass, I think he really will attack us."

"So what are we going to do with him?" Max asked.

Mikey didn't have a chance to answer. He didn't even have a chance to think about it. Suddenly the soda glass was sliding across the table.

The spider was moving again, and the glass moved right along with him.

Before Mikey could react, the glass slid to the edge of the table and went crashing to the floor.

"Watch out!" Max shrieked, jumping up onto one of the chairs in a panic.

Mikey did the same thing. He was sure that the spider was running across the floor, and he was terrified that it was going to run right up his pant leg.

But Mikey was wrong. The spider wasn't on the floor at all. It was clinging to the edge of the table, baring two razor-sharp fangs.

CHAPTER 5

"He's got fangs!" Max cried. "That little sucker has fangs!"

The spider's eyes shifted back and forth between Mikey and Max as if it were deciding which one of them to sink its fangs into first.

But the spider didn't attack either one of them. Instead, it dropped from the table and tore out of the room.

Mikey looked at Max. Max looked at Mikey. Mikey was about to say something when the most horrifying sound cut through the air.

Yeeeeee-ooooooowwwwww! Raaaaarrrrrreeee! It was like nothing Mikey had ever heard before. It was loud and ferocious, almost unearthly, and it was coming from the foyer.

"What the heck is that?" Max gasped.

Mikey's heart stopped, but the sound didn't.

"You don't think it's the spider, do you?" Max asked nervously.

"Spiders don't growl," Mikey shot back. At least he hoped not.

Another loud, wailing yowl tore through the house.

"Uh-oh," Mikey said. "I think it's Fluffy."

Max swallowed hard. "Do we have to go check on her?"

Mikey nodded. He didn't want to go either. With the way Fluffy was carrying on, who knew what they'd find? He inched his way into the foyer, with Max right behind him.

Fluffy was backed into the corner opposite the stairs. Her back was arched and her fur stood on end, making her look three times her normal size. Her teeth were bared, and she was yowling and hissing, spitting up a storm.

"What's wrong with her?" Max whispered.

Mikey was too horrified to answer. He just pointed.

The black spider stood on the floor in front of Fluffy. *Its* hair was on end too!

Mikey blinked. It wasn't the spider's hair that made it look three times its size. The horrible creature was actually growing!

In less than two minutes flat, the spider had grown from the size of a dime to the size of a Ping-Pong ball!

"Geez, oh, man," Max yelped. "He's getting bigger!"

"I know," Mikey cried back.

"How is that possible?" Max asked. "He's supposed to be dead!"

Fluffy let out another wail.

"Get it, you stupid cat!" Mikey screamed at the terrified fur ball.

But the cat didn't move. She didn't even look at Mikey. She just kept her eyes on the spider, yowling all the while.

The spider began creeping toward Fluffy, backing her deeper and deeper into the corner.

"You don't think he can really hurt her, do you, Max?" Mikey asked.

But before Max could say anything, Mikey got his answer.

Fluffy swiped at the spider with her paw. That was a terrible mistake. The spider buried its horrible fangs deep into Fluffy's leg.

Fluffy let out a screech, then shot straight up into the air as if she'd been fired from a cannon. She flew over the spider and raced up the stairs, leaving a trail of blood droplets behind her.

"Did you see that?" Mikey gasped.

"I told you that thing was a man-eater!" Max yelped, backing away.

"Fluffy's a cat, not a man, you moron," Mikey pointed out. He was trying to stay calm. "And the spider didn't exactly eat her either."

"What are you talking about? He just took a huge chunk of flesh out of her leg!" Max jumped in. "If Fluffy hadn't run away, who knows what other body parts that zombie spider would have tried to chow down on!"

Mikey didn't have a chance to respond. The spider had turned around, and now it was coming toward them.

Max saw it too. "Step on him!" Max said, pushing Mikey toward the spider.

"No way!" Mikey was afraid to go anywhere near it.

"Come on," Max urged Mikey. "He can't bite you the way he bit Fluffy. You've got heavy work boots on."

Max was right. There was no way that spider could chomp through an inch of rubber sole.

Mikey moved quickly, before he could lose his courage. He walked right up to the spider, lifted his foot, and brought it crashing down on the horrid creature.

But Mikey got a big surprise. The spider didn't squash. The creature felt hard under Mikey's foot, as though Mikey had stepped on a huge marble instead of a spider.

Mikey was afraid to take his foot away—until eight hairy black legs shot out from under his work boot.

"Look out!" Mikey screamed, jumping away from the spider.

Max jumped back too.

The spider just stood there, staring at them both, baring its bloody fangs.

Suddenly Mikey knew what to do. He raced past the spider and grabbed the front door.

"Good thinking," Max called. "I bet he's dying to go outside."

But the spider didn't look as if it was leaving any time soon.

"Shoo!" Max said, stomping his foot on the floor.

The spider didn't budge.

"Throw something at it," Mikey suggested.

Max fished around in his pocket and came out with some change. He threw a penny at the spider.

The penny hit it dead on—then bounced right off. Still the spider didn't move.

Max threw another coin with the same results. Then another.

"He's not going anywhere," Max told Mikey.

But Max was wrong.

A white, stringy thread shot out from the spider's red-speckled body. It looked like a strand of dental floss being pulled from its spool, only thicker and shinier. The thread flew over Mikey's head and wrapped itself around the railing on the second floor.

Mikey watched, amazed. But his amazement quickly turned to horror as the spider's body rose from the floor.

The flesh-eating spider was dangling from the end of its web string—right in front of Mikey's face!

CHAPTER 6

Mikey jerked his head back so fast, he banged it against the door.

Max plastered himself against the wall. "This guy is big trouble!" he said, staring up at the dangling spider.

"I told you not to open that stupid jar!" Mikey shot back, rubbing his throbbing skull.

"He was dead!" Max screamed. "Remember? This is all your fault!"

"My fault?" Mikey couldn't believe what he was hearing. "How is it my fault?"

"Because you're the one who had the stupid dissecting kit in the first place!" Max declared. "Not me!"

"This is just great," Mikey said. "A killer spider is dangling from a web string right above our heads, and you want to pick a fight with me."

"Just forget I said it, okay?" Max replied. "Let's just get rid of him!"

"Like how?" Mikey demanded.

But Max was stumped too.

The spider wasn't all that far over their heads, just far enough to be out of reach. Not that Mikey would have dared to touch it anyway.

"I've got an idea," Mikey told Max. "You stay here and keep an eye on him. I'll go and get some bug spray."

"Cool!" Max said. "We can terminate him!"

"Yeah," Mikey agreed. "Ex-terminate him." It was the perfect solution. With bug spray, they wouldn't have to get anywhere near the little monster to kill it.

"Hurry up," Max called as Mikey took off.

Mikey's mom kept things like bug spray and cleaning products in a closet in the laundry room. But when Mikey pulled open the door, there wasn't a can of bug spray to be seen. He tore the closet apart looking for something that would help him—something that had the word "bug" on it anywhere. But there was nothing but tons of cleaning products.

Mikey slammed the closet door shut in frustration. *Now what?*

He was about to walk away when a new idea hit him.

His mother was always saying that you had to be careful with cleaning products. Some of them were poison. There had to be something in that closet that could kill one stupid, ugly bug!

Mikey threw open the door again and started grabbing

every spray can in sight. Then he dashed back into the foyer.

"He hasn't moved an inch," Max said, looking up at the spider.

"Good." Mikey knelt down and dumped half a dozen spray cans onto the carpet. "Have I got a surprise for him."

Max started picking through the cans. "Where's the bug spray?" he asked.

"We don't have any," Mikey told him. "But there's got to be something in one of these cans that will kill him."

"I hope so," Max said. He didn't sound too convinced.

"Let's try this one." Mikey picked up the can of air freshener. "This stuff is really horrible. Whenever my mother sprays it around the house, I feel like *I'm* going to die."

Mikey snapped off the lid. But before he could spray the air freshener, the spider raced up its web string to the second floor.

"He's not going to get away that easily," Mikey declared.

Mikey headed for the stairs with his spray can. But by the time he reached the top step, the spider had dropped down again.

Mikey ran down the steps. He was only halfway to the bottom when the spider shot up again.

"I think he's trying to psych you out," Max said.

"Don't be stupid," Mikey replied. "He's just a bug."

"Yeah," Max cut in. "A big, scary bug with fangs!"

"Yeah," Mikey agreed. "But he's still a bug. He can't think. And he certainly can't psych me out!" At least that's what Mikey tried to assure himself.

Mikey headed for the top of the stairs. The spider came down.

"Okay, that's it." Mikey stomped to the bottom of the stairs and headed for the spray cans. He was getting so mad, he was beginning to forget all about being scared. He grabbed one of the cans and shoved it into Max's hands.

"You stand here," he told Max, pointing to a spot on the floor that was right under the spider. "I'm going back up. If he comes back down, you blast away."

"Good thinking." Max held his spray can ready to shoot.

Mikey headed up the stairs, feeling smug. "Let's see what that stupid bug does now."

The spider wasn't so stupid.

It waited until Mikey reached the top of the stairs. Then it shot over the balcony onto the second floor and crept out of sight.

CHAPTER 7

"Where did the spider go?" Max shouted.

"Into the bathroom," Mikey answered, racing for the bathroom door. "We've got him trapped!"

Without even looking inside, Mikey slammed the bathroom door shut. "I'm a whole lot smarter than a bug any day," he gloated.

"I don't think so." Max shook his head as he reached the top of the steps.

"What are you talking about?" Mikey asked.

Max answered Mikey's question with one of his own. "Why did you do that, you moron?"

"Do what?"

"Shut the bathroom door," Max explained.

Mikey rolled his eyes at Max's stupid question. "To trap him, you jerk."

"What good does that do us?" Max shot back. "Unless we never have to go to the bathroom again."

Mikey saw his point. Sooner or later somebody was going to have to use that bathroom. "I guess we're going to have to go in there and get him," Mikey said.

"Not me, pal," Max told him. "That spider's probably in there right now, trying to psych us out again. I bet he knows we have to come in there, and he's hanging right inside that door. The minute we open it, he'll bite off our faces or do something worse."

"He is not," Mikey insisted. Still, Mikey wasn't about to take any chances. "Go downstairs and get all the spray stuff," he told Max.

"Now what?" Max asked as he came back upstairs with the cans.

"We're going in, just like the cops on TV," Mikey answered.

Mikey still had the air freshener in his hand. He reached out and grabbed another spray can from Max. It was furniture polish.

"Make sure you have a spray can in each hand," Mikey told Max. "As soon as I open the door, start blasting away."

"How are you going to open the door without a free hand?" Max asked.

Mikey didn't have an answer for that. But Max did.

"Kick it in," he told Mikey. "Just like they do on TV. I'll stay right behind you and cover your back."

"Good idea," Mikey agreed. "Ready?"

Max didn't look too ready. But he nodded anyway.

Mikey lifted his foot and hit the door like a ninja. He was surprised at how easily it flew open. He was also surprised when it smashed against the wall and the doorknob went right through the plaster. But there was no time to think about that. There was a killer spider on the loose and Mikey was determined to get it.

Mikey entered the bathroom with both spray cans blasting. Max was right behind him, spraying everything in sight. Within seconds, the mist inside the bathroom was so thick, Mikey began to cough.

"Stop for a minute," he told Max.

They both stopped spraying and looked around as the air started to clear. There was no sign of the spider.

"Where can he be?" Mikey asked.

Max just shrugged.

Mikey started searching every inch of the floor. But Max's attention was elsewhere.

"Your mom's going to clobber you when she sees this," Max said, looking at the doorknob that was stuck in the wall. He gave it a tug, but it wouldn't budge. He pulled harder.

The doorknob popped out. Plaster crumbled down the wall.

"Oh, no," Mikey groaned. "Let me see." As he pushed Max out of the way, the door shut.

"This is terrible," Mikey said, running his hand over the hole in the wall. Not only was the plaster cracked, his mother's brand-new wallpaper was ruined. She was sure to have a fit.

"You shouldn't have kicked it so hard," Max pointed out.

"You're the one who told me to do it!" Mikey complained.

"Yeah, but I didn't tell you to kick it through the wall!"

Just then Max realized that the door wasn't their only problem. "Uh-oh," he gasped, pointing at the bathroom door while he backed away from it. "We've got company!"

The big black spider was standing in the middle of the door, its eyes fixed on Mikey.

Mikey screamed and practically knocked Max over as he jumped away from the door.

"We've got to get out of here!" Max insisted.

But just as he said it, the spider skittered down the door and perched on the knob.

Mikey swallowed hard.

Now *they* were the ones who were trapped.

CHAPTER 8

"Uh-oh," Max whispered, backing as far away from the spider as he could get. "Something tells me he's not gonna let us out of here!"

"He's a spider!" Mikey snapped. "It's not like he can hold us prisoners!" Mikey had had enough.

"Oh, yeah?" Max said back. "Tell *him* that."

"I will," Mikey said. He wasn't going to let a dumb spider terrorize him. He pointed the air freshener can right in the spider's face. "You're dead, mister!"

Mikey started firing away.

But the spider didn't flinch. It didn't even blink one of its eight bulging eyes.

"It's not working!" Mikey cried. "Shoot him with the scrubbing bubbles!"

Max started firing away from across the room.

Thousands of scrubbing bubbles whizzed through the air, attacking the ceiling and the walls before some of them actually hit the door.

Mikey was sure that the bubbles would scrub the little monster to death as the spider's hairy back started fizzing away under an inch of white, foamy froth.

"He's history," Max said, tossing the empty can into the sink.

The second the can hit the sink, scrubbing bubbles went flying. Only they weren't coming from the can. They were coming from the door.

Mikey couldn't believe his eyes. The spider was shaking itself off, just like a dog who'd been given a bath.

"Watch out!" Max screamed as the spider leaped to the floor.

Mikey jumped up onto the counter in a panic. "Do something!" he yelped.

"I can't!" Max cried, hopping onto the toilet. "There are no more scrubbing bubbles. All I've got left is glass cleaner. And that's just going to make him shiny!"

"What happened to the spray wax?" Mikey snapped.

"I dropped it in the hallway," Max informed him.

Just then a long, stringy web shot up to the counter and wrapped itself around the faucet over the sink, inches away from Mikey's legs.

The spider was on its way up.

Mikey reached for the can of hair spray sitting on the other side of the counter. It was Alison's. Mikey only hoped that it would do to the spider what it did to

Alison's hair. Just one spritz of the stuff turned Alison into a helmet head. Her hair became so hard and crunchy, even a tornado couldn't blow it out of place.

Mikey blasted away.

The thick, sticky spray instantly glued the spider to its string.

"You got him!" Max exclaimed. "Keep spraying!"

Mikey did just that until the spider finally dropped to the floor wrapped in a shiny, thick hairspray cocoon.

"Way to go!" Max congratulated Mikey as he jumped down from the toilet. "I think you killed him!"

Mikey thought so too.

The spider was coated with an inch of hairspray, looking just as stiff and as crunchy as Alison's hairdo.

"Pick him up and flush him down the toilet," Mikey told Max as he jumped down from the counter.

"You pick him up," Max argued. "I'm not touching him."

"Just grab him with some tissues," Mikey said.

"You grab him with tissues," Max shot back.

Only nobody had a chance to grab anything. Because the hairspray cocoon started to crack. And there wasn't a beautiful butterfly inside.

In seconds, the spider was up and running again.

"Geez, oh, man!" Max yelped, jumping into the bathtub. "Here he comes again!"

The spider's eyes were fixed on Mikey.

"Throw me my father's shaving cream!" Mikey yelled, leaping onto the counter again.

Max grabbed the can and tossed it.

Mikey let it rip. But the spider kept moving under the mountain of shaving cream. It was climbing up the cabinets.

"Blow on him!" Mikey cried.

Max tried. But he couldn't blow through the shaving cream hump on top of the spider's back.

The spider kept climbing.

"Wait a minute!" Max exclaimed, leaping out of the tub. "I've got an idea!" He grabbed Alison's hair dryer from the cabinet above the toilet and plugged it in.

"Hurry up!" Mikey cried.

Max hit the switch. A stream of hot air hit the spider.

Shaving cream blew across the room in six different directions. But the spider stood perfectly still.

Mikey jumped down from the counter. "You're a genius!" he exclaimed.

"I know," Max shot back. "But I can't stand here blow-drying this sucker all day! Do something!"

Mikey spotted a solution. It was standing right by the toilet bowl.

"What are you going to do?" Max asked.

"I'm going to push him into the garbage pail with the toilet brush," Mikey told Max. "The second I do, get ready to flush, because I'm going to dump him right into the toilet."

Mikey moved fast. It was the only way not to chicken out.

"Now!" Mikey screamed, swatting the spider into the garbage pail.

Max raced to the bowl faster than a speeding bullet.

Mikey dumped the pail.

The spider hit the water just as Max pulled the lever.

Max heaved a sigh of relief as the hairy little monster swirled around the bowl.

But Mikey didn't breathe until it got sucked right down the pipes.

"Yes!" Mikey exclaimed, giving Max a high five.

But soon the clapping of their hands wasn't the only sound that echoed through the bathroom. A gurgling noise rose from the toilet.

As Mikey looked down into the bowl, something shot upward. Mikey screamed in terror as it hit him square in the face.

CHAPTER 9

"*Aaaaaagh!*" Mikey cried, jumping away from the toilet.

Water was shooting up from the bowl into Mikey's face like lava erupting from a volcano.

"Close the lid, Max!" Mikey screamed. "Before there's another a-rack-knee attack!"

Max stuck out his hand to grab the lid. Just as he did, the toilet stopped spitting.

"Is he in there?" Mikey asked, wiping his face with the sleeve of his sweatshirt.

"I don't know," Max said. "And I don't want to know either." He slammed the lid shut.

"Well, we're going to have to find out sooner or later," he told Max. "There's no way I'm sitting down on that thing until I'm sure that spider's not in there waiting to bite my butt!"

"We can just use your mom's bathroom if we have to go," Max declared.

"Not in the middle of the night, we can't," Mikey pointed out. "My mom will yell at us for not using our own bathroom."

"Then I'll hold it in," Max said.

"And what if he climbs out of there? Huh? What then?" Mikey asked.

Max didn't have an answer for that one.

"We have to look," Mikey insisted. "I'll lift the lid," he told Max. "You peek in."

"I'll lift," Max protested. "You peek."

"Fine," Mikey huffed. "Just lift it slowly."

Max lifted the lid with one finger. Then he jumped back as fast as he could while Mikey leaned over to look.

The coast was clear. There was nothing in the bowl but water.

Just to be safe, Mikey flushed the toilet again.

This time there were no explosions. At least not any coming from the toilet. The next explosion would be coming from Mikey's mom when she got a look at the mess in the bathroom.

"Oh, man," Mikey said, as he accidentally stepped into a pile of shaving cream. "My mother's going to kill us."

Every inch of the bathroom was covered with foamy white goo or filmy white froth. Scrubbing bubbles were all over the place, except for the floor, which was coated with hair spray. The air in the room was so freshened, it was hard not to gag.

"Your mom's going to do worse than kill us," Max agreed.

A chill went through Mikey. Facing his mom was a lot more frightening than facing a flesh-eating spider. Especially when his mom was tired. And Mikey was pretty sure she was going to be tired. After all, she'd spent the whole day with Alison. That was enough to make anybody feel exhausted.

They had to clean up. Fast. And they had to do it without any cleaning stuff, because that was all used up.

Mikey tried to scoop some of the bubbles off the walls to clean up the sticky, hair-sprayed tiles. But it didn't work. The scrubbing bubbles were way too tired to scrub.

Mikey had his nose to the floor, so he didn't notice Max wiping down the walls and sopping up the toilet water until it was too late.

"What are you doing?" Mikey yelped the second he saw Max committing the horrible crime.

"Wiping up the water," Max answered.

"Not with them," Mikey cried. Max was sopping up the toilet water all right—but he was doing it with Mikey's mom's fancy towels.

"They're towels," Max shot back. "What else am I supposed to use?"

"Different towels," Mikey moaned. "My mom uses those for decoration. We're not even allowed to wipe our hands on them. Didn't you see that fancy lace on the edges?"

Max shook his head. "Sorry," he mumbled.

Mikey knew there was no point in screaming at Max. His mother would do it for him. Unless, of course, Mikey could figure out how to work the washing machine before she got home.

"I think we're done," Max declared a few minutes later, dropping the soaking-wet towels into the tub.

The toilet water was off the floor. The bubbles were off the walls. The hair spray was no longer in puddles. And the counter was actually kind of shiny.

Yeah, Mikey thought. *The bathroom is pretty much in order. Sticky, but in order.*

The only thing that still stuck out like a sore thumb was the wall. Actually, it stuck in.

"What are we going to do about that hole from the doorknob?" Mikey wailed.

"Don't worry," Max said. "I know how to spackle. Then we can just color it in like the wallpaper."

Mikey shot Max a worried look.

"I know how to do it," Max assured him. "Spackle is kind of like Play-Doh, only white and sticky. All we have to do is smush a glob of it into the hole. Then we can smooth it over with one of those putty knives. It's a piece of cake," he said confidently.

Mikey wasn't so sure. But he figured the wall couldn't possibly look any worse than it already did.

Mikey and Max headed down to the garage to get the can of spackle and the putty knives. But a disgusting sight stopped them dead in their tracks. Frog guts were splattered all over the kitchen.

"Aw, geez," Mikey sighed. "My mom will bite off my head if she sees frog guts on her table. Look at this mess," he went on. "You didn't dissect this guy. You slaughtered him!"

"Let's just clean it up," Max grumbled. He scooped up the guts into a pile with his bare hands. "What should we do with the body parts?"

"I don't know," Mikey answered. "I guess we can just dump everything down the garbage disposal in the sink."

Mikey and Max cleared the table, cramming the dissecting material back into its box. Then they carried the frog remains to the sink.

Max had the guts, Mikey, the legs.

"Oh, man." Mikey cringed as he turned on the water and flipped on the disposal. "This is too gross."

The motor of the garbage disposal hummed loudly as it sucked the blue squiggly thing with the two red blobs on the end down the drain. But as it sucked up one of the slimy legs, the humming turned to a buzz, kind of like a chain saw. Then the sink started backing up with water, and the disposal started burping up guts.

"Uh-oh," Max said. "I think we clogged the sink."

Mikey groaned. He felt like he was about to throw up.

"Don't panic," Max said, turning off the disposal. "Just give me a plunger."

Mikey did just that and Max started plunging his heart out.

The water began to go down, and the garbage disposal started swallowing up the frog guts again.

Who knows? Mikey thought. *Maybe Max really can spackle a wall.*

"See ya later, buddy," Max said as he dropped the last slimy leg down the drain.

Mikey laughed. So did Max. And so did somebody else.

Mikey and Max froze, terrified by the sound.

It wasn't a laugh at all. It was a shriek! And it was coming from the drain.

Something in the pipes was alive.

CHAPTER

10

To Mikey's relief, the shrieks from the sink didn't last very long. In fact, they disappeared a second later, along with the frog guts—and the stainless-steel scalpel that Max had "accidentally" dropped down the drain with the frog's legs.

Those shrieks were just the metal scalpel scraping its way down the drain, Mikey tried to convince himself. Not the sound of some horrible creature screeching its way through the pipes.

Another shriek made him forget all about the one that had come from the drain. It was the one that started in the bathroom the instant his mother got home. The one that had been going on for close to an hour.

"You're dead," Alison taunted them.

"Shut up!" Mikey said, pushing her out of his face. It

wasn't a very clever comeback. But it was the best Mikey could do under the circumstances.

"I've never heard Mommy sound so mad," Alison declared. "What'd you do, anyway?"

"None of your business," Mikey shot back.

But Alison found out soon enough.

"Michael Adam Davis!" Mikey's mom bellowed as she stomped back down the stairs.

Alison smirked, then plunked herself down in her chair, ready to watch the fireworks.

Mrs. Davis charged into the kitchen in a rage. She was huffing and puffing so hard, Mikey could practically see the steam shooting out of her nostrils. And her face was so red, it looked like her whole head was about to explode.

"How could you have done this?" she said. Her voice was barely above a whisper. "How could you have put a hole in the wall?"

"Mom," Mikey started, trying to stay calm. "I know this sounds crazy, but a killer spider was in the bathroom and—"

"Oh, really?" His mother cut him off in a nasty tone. "A killer spider?"

"That's right," Max piped up. "And he was trying to eat us."

Alison hooted loudly. "I can't believe what babies you two are."

"It's true, Mom," Mikey insisted.

"That's the most ridiculous excuse I've ever heard,"

Mrs. Davis snapped, her eyes flashing like fireballs. "You two have ruined my brand-new wallpaper. Now I'm going to have to have the whole bathroom redone. Not to mention that you've ruined my towels and left every inch of that bathroom sticky and smelly. All because of a bug!" She was screaming now. She stormed around the kitchen setting the table. She was so angry, she didn't notice the smoke that was seeping out from the oven door.

Mikey wasn't about to point it out to her either. He was too afraid to make a sound.

It was Alison who finally got up the courage to call it to her mother's attention. "Uh, Mom," Alison muttered, pointing to the oven.

"Oh, no!" Mikey's mom started toward the oven. But halfway there, she slipped on something and nearly fell.

"What on earth was that?" she cried as she grabbed on to the counter to regain her balance. Her eyes blazed with fury when she looked at the floor and saw what it was.

Mikey saw it too. It was a piece of the worm from the dissecting kit, its guts smashed all over the floor.

"A worm!" Mrs. Davis shrieked. "How in the world did this get here?"

Mikey tried to think of the right thing to say. But there was no right thing. Anything that came out of his mouth would only get him into deeper trouble.

Luckily, he didn't have to say anything at all.

"Never mind," his mother said. Now she sounded on the verge of tears. "I don't want to know. I just can't take anymore."

She made her way over to the oven and threw open the door. The chicken that she'd put in earlier was burned to a crisp.

"Dinner's ruined," she announced, looking at Mikey and Max as if that were their fault too. She grabbed her oven mitts, took the pan out of the oven, and dumped the whole chicken into the garbage.

"You two get this trash out of here," she said to Mikey and Max. "Then make yourselves a sandwich, and make yourselves scarce. I don't want to lay eyes on you for the rest of the night."

It looked like Ice Land was totally out of the question now. Their weekend of fun was off to a really rocky start.

"At least the spider's gone," Max mumbled as they headed for the garbage cans out by the garage.

"Yeah," Mikey agreed, trying to look on the bright side. "We flushed him into oblivion—didn't we?"

"That's for sure," Max replied.

But Mikey and Max were wrong. Dead wrong.

CHAPTER 11

Mikey went into the bathroom and locked the door behind him. Tonight he was going to take a long, hot bath instead of a shower. Between his mother's yelling and Max's whining, he had a terrible headache. Every muscle in his body felt like it was twisted into one big knot. A steaming-hot bath was just what he needed. That, and a few minutes of peace and quiet.

Mikey climbed into the bathtub while the water was still running so that he could wash his hair under the faucet. The water was just the right temperature—hot, but not scalding. Mikey started to relax right away.

Suddenly a terrible pounding on the bathroom door snapped him out of it.

"Who is it?" he barked.

"It's me," Max's voice answered. "Let me in."

"I can't," Mikey told him. "I'm in the tub."

"I need to brush my teeth," Max whined.

"I'll be out in a couple of minutes," Mikey said.

"Well, hurry up," Max said.

Mikey ignored him and reached for the shampoo. He stuck his head under the running water. If Max was still talking outside that door, Mikey couldn't hear him anymore.

When Mikey finished wetting his hair, it was quiet out in the hall. Mikey heaved a sigh of relief. He poured some shampoo into the palm of his hand, dumped it onto his head, and started lathering up.

When his hair was squeaky clean, he lay back under the faucet again.

Water poured down over his head. Mikey was in no hurry. He lay there with his eyes closed, daydreaming.

Whaaack!

Something hit Mikey in the center of the forehead. It was small and hard, and it stung.

Mikey sat up fast, rubbing his forehead. He couldn't imagine what had hit him. Whatever it was must have dropped out of the faucet.

He looked around the tub and spotted the problem immediately. It was floating on the surface of the water in front of him. Mikey looked at the object curiously. Then he looked back at the faucet. *That's weird,* he thought.

The object from the faucet looked like a pearl bobbing in the bathwater.

As Mikey reached for it, another one dropped out of the faucet. Then another. And another. Within a few seconds, the whole surface of the bathtub was covered with shiny white beads.

Mikey stuck his hand under the faucet to try and catch a handful of them so that he could inspect them more closely. But the second the beads hit his hand, they started to crack.

Mikey had no idea what was happening. Not until he saw slimy black goo oozing out of the pearly white shells into the palm of his hand.

The beads from the faucet weren't pearls at all! They were eggs! Spider eggs! And they were hatching in Mikey's hand!

Dozens of tiny, black, red-speckled spiders emerged from their shells, as hundreds of little hairy legs tickled Mikey's palm.

Baby killer spiders!

Mikey screamed like crazy as he shook his hand desperately, trying to get the creatures off.

One by one, the flesh-eating babies fell into the tub. Mikey watched in horror as their legs clung to the floating white eggs still waiting to hatch.

Mikey's heart was pounding so hard and so fast, he thought for sure that *it* was about to hatch—right out of his chest!

He had to get out of the tub. He tried to stand up, but he was so panicked his feet slipped out from under him and he plunged into the water.

The bubbles from the shampoo burned his eyes. Mikey tried to rub the sting away as he pulled his face out of the water. But the stinging was nowhere near as horrible as the sensation he felt next.

Every inch of his skin was coming alive!

Hairy little legs were crawling up his spine . . . and down his arms . . . and across his chest. Every pearly white egg had broken wide open.

Mikey was sitting in a sea of baby flesh-eating spiders. And they were crawling all over him.

CHAPTER 12

"Help!" Mikey cried out in panic. "Somebody help me!"

The spiders' legs clung to his flesh as he thrashed around in the bathtub. No matter how hard Mikey tried, he just couldn't get his feet under him. Every time he tried to stand up, he slipped right back down.

Meanwhile the baby spiders kept climbing all over him.

I'm about to become their very first meal! Mikey thought.

"Help me!" he screamed. "Somebody help me!"

But no one heard him. Besides, even if somebody did come, the bathroom door was locked. Mikey would still be stuck in there alone!

Finally, Mikey managed to get to his feet. He leaped

from the bathtub with dozens of spiders still clinging to his flesh.

"Get off me!" he cried. He hopped around the bathroom, flicking wildly at the spiders. They flew everywhere—on the floor, on the walls, on the mirror.

Mikey grabbed his towel, wrapped it around himself, and threw open the bathroom door.

"Max!" he screamed, racing for his bedroom. "Max!"

Mikey shot through his bedroom door and slammed right into Max.

"Ouch!" Max cried, rubbing his head. "What's wrong with you? You almost cracked my skull open!"

"Spiders!" Mikey told him frantically. "They were coming out of the faucet! They're all over the bathroom!"

"What are you shouting about now?" another voice asked.

Mikey spun toward the sound of it.

It was his mother. She was standing in the doorway with her arms folded in front of her, not looking the least bit happy.

"Just follow me," Mikey told her. "I'll show you."

Mikey rushed past his mother, out into the hallway. Max was right behind him.

"What's going on around here?" Alison asked, coming out of her own room.

"You'll see," Mikey told her.

He stopped in the hallway in front of the bathroom door. "In there," he said, pointing.

Mrs. Davis shot him a look that said, "This had better

be good." Then she moved toward the open door.

Mikey watched as she peeked inside the bathroom. Now he could prove once and for all that he and Max had been telling the truth.

Sure enough, he saw the look of horror that came over her face. He heard her gasp.

"See, Mom?" he said, coming up beside her, close enough to see into the bathroom himself.

Then Mikey gasped too. His problems had just gotten much, much worse.

CHAPTER 13

There wasn't one single spider in the bathroom. But the water in the bathtub was overflowing onto the floor. And Mikey's mother was furious.

She sloshed through the water to the tub and turned off the tap. Then she just stood there, glaring at Mikey, vibrating with rage.

"There were spiders in here, Mom," he said weakly. "I swear."

Mrs. Davis opened her mouth. But no words came out. She just made sputtering sounds.

Finally she said through clenched teeth, "Just go to your room. And stay there. If I hear another peep out of you or Max tonight, I'm going to nail that bedroom door shut from the outside. Do you understand me?"

Mikey just nodded.

"And tomorrow," she went on, "don't even think about Ice Land. Tomorrow, the two of you are going to be very busy. You are going to rake all the leaves in the yard, and you are going to wash my car. That should keep you out of trouble."

Mikey could hear Alison snickering. But there was nothing he could do about it.

"Go!" his mother boomed, pointing toward his room.

Mikey and Max took off. They ducked into Mikey's room and closed the door behind them.

"This is too weird," Mikey said, still shaken. "There were millions of spiders and spider eggs in that bathroom. Where did they all go?"

"Are you sure you didn't just imagine the whole thing?" Max said.

"No way," Mikey told him, plunking himself down on his bed. "I'm telling you, there were millions of them crawling all over the place."

"Then where are they?" Max sat on the twin bed across the room. He was facing Mikey.

"I don't have a clue," Mikey replied. He cast his eyes around the room, nervously checking for tiny spiders. Just the thought that they might be crawling around on the floor somewhere made Mikey pull his feet up onto the bed. Fast.

Max did the same thing.

A knock on the door made them both jump.

Mikey didn't have time to ask who it was before the door flew open.

"Do you two jerks have Fluffy in here?" Alison demanded.

Fluffy! Mikey hadn't thought about the cat since the spider attacked her. He hadn't seen her since then either. That was a problem. But he wasn't about to share that information with Alison.

"No, your stupid froufrou cat is not in here!" he shot back.

"I can't find her anywhere," Alison complained. "If you two little weasels have done anything to her . . ." Alison didn't finish her threat. She just slammed the door and stomped off.

Mikey and Max looked at one another.

"You don't think the spiders ate Fluffy, do you?" Max whispered.

"No way," Mikey said, forcing a laugh. "We're talking about teeny tiny *baby* spiders, Max."

"Yeah," Max shot back. "Teeny tiny *flesh-eating* spiders, remember? Flesh-eating spiders that could sneak in here in the middle of the night and eat us too!"

"That's not going to happen," Mikey said. But he didn't believe his words, not for a second.

Neither did Max. "We have to do something to protect ourselves," he said.

"Like what?" Mikey asked.

"I don't know." Max shrugged. "There's got to be something we can do."

"Something that won't get us into trouble with my mom," Mikey said.

"I've got it!" Max declared.

"What?" Mikey asked.

"It's perfect," Max said, sounding awfully proud of himself. "Actually, it's brilliant. Wait until you hear."

Mikey rolled his eyes. "Just tell me already!"

"Okay," Max said finally. "The first thing we have to do is push our beds into the center of the room."

"Huh?" Mikey already didn't like this idea one bit.

"Just listen to me," Max insisted. "We're going to build a defense. Just like a moat around a castle, or a soldier's foxhole. Only we're going to use the duct tape!"

"You're crazy," Mikey said, shaking his head.

"It'll work," Max insisted. "I swear."

"That's what you said about kicking the bathroom door in too," Mikey reminded him.

"Fine," Max huffed as he got up to start pushing his own bed. "Get eaten. See if I care."

Mikey had no choice but to go along with Max's plan, since he didn't have one of his own.

Together, Mikey and Max pushed both beds into the center of the room, side by side.

"Now what?" Mikey asked.

Max was already a step ahead of him. He grabbed the two-sided tape out of the pile of junk that had been under Mikey's bed.

"Now we surround the beds with this tape," Max responded to Mikey's question.

"What's that going to do?" Mikey asked.

"It's going to keep the spiders away," Max answered.

He was already laying tape. "Don't you get it?" he went on. "The tape is sticky on both sides. It will stick to the carpet. And if anything tries to cross over it, like one of those killer spiders, it will get stuck, since the tape's sticky on top too."

Mikey hated to admit it, but the plan *was* brilliant.

"Good thinking!" He high-fived Max. Then he helped him construct a duct-tape moat around both their beds. To be extra safe, they also stuck tape around the edges of their comforters.

"Maybe we ought to go put some tape down around your mom's bed too," Max suggested.

Mikey thought about it for a second. He certainly didn't want his mom to get eaten by spiders. But he didn't want to get yelled at either. "We better not," Mikey told him. "She'll just scream at us again."

"What about Alison?" Max snickered. "What if the spiders get into her bed?"

Mikey snickered too. He suddenly had an idea. "Maybe we should put some lunch meat outside Alison's door so that the spiders *will* go straight to her room!"

Max loved the idea. "Let's do it!" he said.

Mikey wanted to. But the thought of his mother catching them was way too scary. "Nah," Mikey said. "We'll only get in more trouble."

"Well, at least *we'll* be able to sleep peacefully," Max said as he climbed into bed.

Mikey nodded. Only he wasn't so sure.

"See you in the morning." Max yawned and pulled the

covers up around him. He was asleep before Mikey had even turned out the light.

Mikey only wished that he was as convinced as Max was that they were safe. He kept his eyes on the floor, watching for any sign of spiders. But there was none.

Still, Mikey kept watching. It felt as though he watched for hours. He fought to keep his eyes open.

Maybe we are safe, Mikey thought, yawning sleepily. *Max was right. There's nothing to worry about. No way the spiders are going to get to us . . .*

Mikey began to doze off.

Suddenly he was startled by shadows creeping across his bed. Terror gripped his heart as he realized that watching the floor had been a terrible mistake.

CHAPTER 14

Mikey looked up in horror. Millions of baby spiders were creeping across the ceiling on billions of legs!

"Maaaaaaaxxxxxx!" Mikey cried in a panic. "Wake up!"

Max didn't budge.

"Get up, you idiot!" Mikey hollered. "We have to get out of here! The ceiling is covered with the killer babies from the bathtub!"

Max still didn't move. But the ceiling did. Pieces of plaster started falling.

"Oh, no!" Mikey cried. The ceiling was caving in. Mikey waited for the tiny man-eating spiders to fall down with it onto his bed!

But he was wrong. All of a sudden, the spiders above him parted down the middle and ran down the walls.

Mikey was frozen with terror. *Please don't let them*

climb into my bed! he pleaded. *Please let them get stuck in the tape.*

As the baby spiders crept across the carpet, another piece of plaster dropped from above. The biggest, hairiest spider leg burst right through the plaster!

Mikey opened his mouth to scream, but he couldn't make a sound. Fear took total control. Mikey's body went stiff as a board.

The giant spider leg started sawing away at the ceiling in a circle. It almost looked like a cartoon. But Mikey wasn't laughing—especially when a piece of plaster the size of a manhole cover crashed to the bed, landing right on top of Max.

Max rolled over without even opening his eyes.

Mikey couldn't believe it. Max was about to die and he didn't even know it!

A-rack-knee-a-whatever-it-was was climbing out of the ceiling. It was big enough to eat them both!

"Noooooooooooooo!" Mikey cried.

A web string the thickness of a rope shot straight from the spider's black, hairy body and landed splat in the middle of Mikey's face. It was wet and sticky, and it stung. The second it hit Mikey's face it stuck fast to his skin. Mikey tried to pull it away. The web string was so thick he had to use two hands. And the moment he touched it, all ten of his fingers stuck to it—just like his face.

The baby spiders started circling the bed as another sticky, wet string shot down from above. This one wrapped itself around Mikey's ankles.

One string after another shot down from the ceiling and lassoed his body. Mikey was being roped and tied like a fat, juicy steer in a rodeo show!

Please don't eat me. Mikey's eyes were pleading with the spider as he peered through the web strings that covered his face.

But the eight bulging black eyeballs glaring down at him showed no mercy.

Mikey couldn't watch. He was sure that the horrible creature was preparing to rip off his flesh and pass it out to the creepy crawly crowd on the floor.

But just as he closed his eyes, a horrified voice shrieked through the air.

"Michael!"

It sounded so close. And it sounded so familiar!

"Mom!" Mikey cried back. But it came out all muffled. His mouth was covered with sticky white webs. He could barely pull his lips apart.

"Mi-chael!" His mother cried again. This time she sounded even closer.

Mom's here to save me! Mikey thought to himself in relief. *No way she's going to let a bunch of killer spiders eat me. She's going to kick their spider butts!*

Suddenly Mikey felt his whole body being lifted from the bed. His mother was scooping him up. She was pulling him away from the giant spider! Mikey was sure of it!

But Mikey was wrong. It wasn't his mom at all. It was

the spider! The giant, hairy beast was lifting Mikey off the bed like a yo-yo cocoon on a string.

"Oh, no!" Mikey's mother's voice sounded even more panicked than before. And Mikey knew why. The spider was opening its mouth.

Through the sticky white webs that covered his eyes, Mikey could see its razor-sharp fangs ready to chow down.

CHAPTER 15

"*Mi-chael!*"

Mikey's mom screamed so loud, she even scared the spider.

The spider let go! He wasn't about to mess with Mikey's mom!

Mikey felt himself roll through the air as the spider's thick, heavy web started to unravel. He hit the bed hard, but he was still trapped in the sticky cocoon. There was no way for him to jump from the bed and run. He tried to roll, but he couldn't. He stuck to the sheets like a fly stuck to fly paper.

Mikey twisted like crazy. But before he could twist himself free, he felt himself going back up again, bed sheets and all.

The spider was yanking Mikey up to its mouth.

"Get him, Mom!" Mikey screamed.

"It's you I'm going to get!" Mikey's mother screamed back. Her voice wasn't reassuring at all. In fact, it was kind of scary.

"Michael Adam Davis!" his mother shouted again. "Wake up!"

Terror tore through Mikey's heart. His mother wasn't screaming at the spider. She was screaming at him.

Mikey's eyes popped wide open. And there weren't any web strings protecting his face from the two bulging eyes that glared back at him.

The killer spiders were gone. But the killer mom sitting on the edge of his bed was real. The look on her face told Mikey that he was waking up to an even bigger nightmare.

"What have you done now?" Mrs. Davis shrieked.

"What do you mean?" Mikey asked, sitting up and gazing around the room. There wasn't a spider in sight. And there was no way he could have done anything bad yet. He wasn't even out of bed.

"What do I mean?" She repeated Mikey's question.

That always spelled trouble. Mikey braced himself for the fireworks.

"What I mean is your carpet," she growled. Then she pulled up a piece of the duct tape. "Look at this, Michael!"

Mikey swallowed hard as he stared at the green, fuzzy strands of carpeting clinging to the tape.

"By the time I get all of this tape up," Mrs. Davis complained, "half of your carpet will be gone. And it's going to take me all day to scrub the sticky stuff off whatever's left of this rug!"

Mikey looked to Max for help. But Max wasn't about to open his eyes. In fact, he was squeezing them shut as hard as he could.

"I'm sorry, Mom," Mikey apologized. "I didn't know that would happen."

"What did you think was going to happen when you put duct tape all over the carpet?" she demanded.

Mikey shrugged.

"Answer my question," she said.

Mikey took a deep breath to steady his nerves. Then he started to confess. "Max said the killer spiders would get stuck to the duct tape. That way, they couldn't attack us while we were sleeping."

Max sprang up like a shot to defend himself. "You're the one who said it was a good idea!"

Mikey's mom didn't care whose fault it was. She was mad either way.

"If I hear any more nonsense about spiders," she warned, "I'll ground you for life. Do you understand?"

"But, Mom," Mikey protested. "There really are killer spiders in this house!"

"I mean it, Michael," she said, turning her attention to the carpet. "I don't want to hear the 's' word again. Now get out of here so I can clean up this mess."

Mikey and Max weren't about to argue. Besides, Mikey's stomach was growling up a storm. He had a craving for French toast, but he didn't think it would be such a good idea to ask his mom to cook—at least not right now. So he and Max headed for the kitchen to dig through some cereal boxes.

"I hope you have Popplers," Max said as they made their way through the foyer. "I love that cereal."

"Me too!" Mikey agreed. "But my mom won't buy it. She says it's loaded with junk."

"Aw, man," Max whined. "What kind of cereal do you have?"

Mikey had no choice but to drop the bomb. "Healthy stuff," he told Max.

Max looked like he'd just been given the worst news of his life. "You're kidding me, right?"

Mikey shook his head.

"You mean like gross, healthy stuff?" Max cringed.

Mikey nodded again. "You know what, though?" he said. "I think we have some Krispies!"

"Krispies are cool!" Max sounded relieved as he followed Mikey into the kitchen. "I can definitely go for some Krispies."

The second Mikey hit the tiled floor, he stopped dead in his tracks. He and Max weren't the only ones who wanted Krispies! Standing in the middle of the kitchen was a big, hairy beast with long, hairy legs. It had already beaten them to the cereal cabinet.

CHAPTER 16

"*Aaaaaaaaggggggh!*" Max screamed. "It lives!"

"And boy, is it ugly!" Mikey added, covering his eyes.

"Look who's talking!" the creature growled, pouring some Krispies into a bowl.

"No wonder your sister spends six hours in the bathroom every day," Max said. "She's definitely scary looking in the morning."

Mikey laughed. Alison *was* a scary sight. Her helmet head must have cracked open while she was sleeping, because her hair was shooting up in twelve different directions. And her froufrou pajamas must have shrunk in the wash, because her legs were sticking out of the bottom of them like a fuzzy pair of stilts.

Mikey couldn't even bring himself to look down at her feet. Alison wasn't wearing slippers, and Mikey had no desire to see her long, ugly toes right before he ate. Mikey was sure Alison's toes were so long, she'd fit right in at the zoo with the monkeys.

He pointed them out to Max.

"Oh, gross." Max cringed, following Mikey's finger to Alison's feet. "Put some combat boots on those gunboats," he told Alison.

Mikey cracked up.

"Shut up," Alison growled back. "At least I know which end of my body to sit on," she said.

"What's that supposed to mean?" Max asked.

"It means you're a butt face," Alison sneered. "So how come you guys aren't wearing your Spider-Man pajamas?" she teased as she headed to the refrigerator.

"Very funny," Mikey snapped.

"I mean, if you're gonna fight spiders," Alison laughed, grabbing the milk, "shouldn't you dress up?"

"You're such a jerk!" Max said exactly what Mikey was thinking.

Just then the phone rang.

Alison tried to grab it. But Mikey shoved her out of the way.

"I bet I know who this is," he teased, picking up the portable receiver.

"Give me that!" Alison demanded.

Mikey wasn't about to.

"Hello," he said into the receiver.

The voice on the other end was exactly the voice Mikey was expecting. The voice of Alison's goofy, pimply-faced boyfriend. "Is Alison there?"

"Who is it?" Alison demanded.

Mikey ignored her. "No," he said back into the receiver. "Alison's not here right now, Ed-die. But she told me to tell you how much she *loooooooooooves* you."

"Give me that phone!" Alison barked. She slammed the milk carton down on the counter and ripped the receiver from Mikey's hand.

Mikey and Max cracked up as Alison stormed into the other room to get some privacy.

"She wants to marry you, Ed-die!" Mikey screamed as loud as he could so that Alison's boyfriend would hear him.

Max kept laughing as he reached for the box of cereal Alison had left on the counter. "Oh, man," he groaned, looking into the empty box. "You're all out of Krispies!"

"Eat Alison's," Mikey told him.

"Good idea," Max agreed. He grabbed Alison's bowl and reached for the milk. But as he lifted the carton, something stopped him from pouring. He cocked his ear toward the bowl instead. "Hey, Mikey," he said. "I thought these things weren't supposed to snap, crackle, and pop until you put milk on them."

Mikey heard it too. "That's too weird," he said, staring down into the bowl.

Suddenly the cereal started to do more than snap, crackle, and pop. It started to move! Dozens of tiny black blobs speckled with red started climbing out of the bowl.

"Spiders!" Max yelped, jumping away from the counter

79

as the bugs skittered over the edge and onto the floor.

Alison stormed back into the room. "I'm telling Mommy what a jerk you were," she said, slamming the receiver back into its cradle.

"Alison!" Mikey yelped as dozens of hairy legs scrambled toward her toes. "Watch out! There's a bunch of killer spiders right behind you!"

"Yeah, right," Alison said. She didn't even turn around.

"There is!" Max cried. "Look down, you idiot!"

The baby spiders crawled right past Alison's feet and disappeared into a crack in the floor board.

By the time Alison looked down, there wasn't a spider in sight.

"You two need serious help," Alison said, heading for the bowl of Krispies on the counter. She picked up the milk and started to pour. Then she reached into the drawer and grabbed a spoon.

"What are you doing?" Mikey cried as Alison stuck the spoon into the bowl. "You can't eat that cereal! It's full of spider eggs!"

"So's your head," Allison said, cramming the spoon into her mouth.

Max grabbed his stomach like he was going to puke.

Mikey watched in horror as his sister chomped down on a mouthful of Krispie-covered spider eggs.

CHAPTER 17

"What do you suppose is going to happen to Alison?" Max asked, shouting over the sound of the leaf blower.

Mikey just shrugged and shook his head. He didn't want to think about it. He kept on raking.

The two of them were working on the front lawn. They'd flipped a coin to decide who would rake first and who got to use the leaf blower. Max won. But he wasn't doing a very good job.

"You're supposed to help me get the leaves into a pile," Mikey hollered at him. "Not blow the pile I've raked all over the yard again."

"I'm doing the best I can," Max defended himself.

But he wasn't. Max wasn't even paying attention to what he was doing. He was too busy talking about Alison.

"Something's got to happen to her," Max insisted.

"Nothing's going to happen," Mikey said. Only he wasn't so sure. He'd seen her eat the eggs with his very own eyes.

"What if all those spider eggs hatch inside her?" Max asked. "What if her whole body explodes into spiders?"

Mikey actually laughed. "What if she just turns into one giant spider?" he offered.

"Then she'd be uglier than she already is." Max laughed too.

"Not by much," Mikey added. He dropped his rake onto the ground and headed toward the garage to get some bags. He figured it was time to start bagging the one pile he'd managed to rake before Max blew it all away again.

There were garbage cans right outside the garage door. As Mikey passed by them, he heard a sound coming from one of them. He backed up to listen.

A crunching sound was coming from inside the can where he and Max had thrown last night's dinner—the burnt chicken.

An uneasy feeling started in Mikey's stomach. "Hey, Max!" he shouted. "Come here."

Max turned off the leaf blower and headed over to Mikey. The crunching was getting much louder.

"What is that?" Max asked, looking suspiciously at the garbage can.

"Let's find out," Mikey said. "Stand back," he warned Max. He knocked the lid off the can and jumped away.

"Look at that!" Max gasped.

The trash bag inside the can was moving. There was something alive inside the bag.

"Put the lid back on!" Max shouted.

But before Mikey could even bend over to pick up the lid, the garbage can toppled over and the bag rolled out onto the driveway. It was moving. And bulging. And crunching.

Mikey and Max started to back away.

Mikey was about to turn and run when the bag exploded. Garbage went flying everywhere. But that wasn't the only thing that came out of the bag.

Mikey watched in horror as hundreds of spiders tumbled out of the mess. Each one scurried across the driveway in a different direction. Within seconds, they disappeared into the grass.

But it was what they left behind that really frightened Mikey.

"Look at that!" Mikey gasped, pointing to what was on the ground in front of them.

"Holy smokes!" Max exclaimed. "Is that last night's chicken?"

"It *was*," Mikey answered.

There wasn't a bit of meat left anywhere. Just bones. They were picked so clean that they looked as though they'd been bleached by the desert sun.

"Those spiders really are flesh-eaters," Max said nervously.

And now they were everywhere.

CHAPTER 18

There wasn't a spider to be seen when Mikey's mother came out the front door with Alison. But there was garbage everywhere.

"I'm not even going to ask," Mrs. Davis said coldly.

Alison stood behind her, making faces at Mikey.

"Alison and I are going food shopping," Mikey's mother informed them. "This mess had better not be here when we get back."

Mikey wanted to tell his mother that he and Max had not made the mess. But there was no way Mikey was going to say the word "spider" to his mother. There was no point. She was never going to believe them.

"Get to it," Mrs. Davis snapped as she started for the car.

Mikey turned and headed into the garage to get the trash bags. Max was right on his heels.

"Your sister is such a jerk," Max complained. "Did you see the way she was smirking at us? She even stuck her tongue out when your mom wasn't looking. Didn't you notice that? How come Alison never gets in trouble? She's the mean one."

Max would have gone on, but Mikey shut him up. "Listen to that," he said.

It sounded like crying.

"Where's it coming from?" Max asked, looking around.

"Somewhere in the garage," Mikey answered. He started looking around, too, moving things to check beneath them.

"Oh, my gosh!" Max exclaimed. "You don't think somebody left a baby in here, do you?" Max always jumped to the most amazing conclusions.

"It's not a baby," Mikey assured him.

"It sure sounds like one," Max insisted.

It did sound like a baby. For a moment even Mikey began to think it was, but then he realized what they were really hearing.

"It's froufrou cat," Mikey exclaimed.

"So what's she crying about?" Max asked. Then it dawned on him and Mikey.

They both started looking furiously.

"Fluffy!" they called out in unison. "Fluffy! Where are you?"

A long, loud wail answered their cries. They followed the sound all the way to the back of the garage, where they finally found Fluffy.

Mikey gasped when he saw where she was.

Fluffy the froufrou cat was in the corner of the garage, up near the ceiling, trapped like a bug in the biggest spiderweb Mikey had ever seen.

CHAPTER 19

Froufrou cat was about to be dinner. Mikey was sure of it.

"We have to do something!" he exclaimed. "We can't just leave her up there."

"Why not?" Max asked, looking around the garage as if he was expecting something to jump out at him.

"Because she'll end up just like those chicken bones," Mikey informed him.

"No way I'm staying in here!" Max told Mikey. "Whoever built this web is coming back. And I'm not sticking around to see which one of us he wants to eat for dessert!"

Max had a point.

The web was so big that Fluffy looked like a fly in the center of it, only poofy and white. The spider that built the sticky trap for Fluffy had to be big—bigger than Fluffy. Maybe even as big as the spider in Mikey's dream!

Mikey wanted to get out of the garage too. Fast. But as he started to run, Fluffy started to meow.

If it had been Alison dangling from the web, Mikey might have left her. But her stupid cat sounded so helpless, Mikey couldn't turn his back.

"We have to save her," Mikey insisted.

"Why?" Max cried. "I thought you hated that cat."

"I do," Mikey told him. "But my mother will kill us if she finds out we let a giant spider eat Alison's cat."

Then Mikey had a thought. "Wait a minute," he said. "Maybe we *should* leave Fluffy up there. That way we can prove to my mother that there really are killer spiders in the house!"

"Good idea," Max agreed. "Now let's get out of here!"

But the second Mikey turned his back, Fluffy let out another pitiful cry. Mikey felt like a criminal. "Okay," he huffed, looking up at Fluffy. "I'll get you down."

Mikey knew it was the right thing to do. Maybe he could still show his mom the giant web and convince her of the spiders that way.

Max had no choice but to help.

Fluffy was so high up, they needed a ladder to reach her.

Mikey climbed while Max stood guard, watching for signs of killer spiders.

Pulling Fluffy from the web was like trying to pull bubble gum from the bottom of a sneaker.

Every time Mikey yanked the cat, Fluffy bounced back into the web. The only thing that came off were long, gooey strings and patches of fur balls with dead flies stuck all over them.

"It's no use," Mikey moaned. "There's no way I can rip through these strings. They're too sticky and thick."

"Try the hedge clippers," Max suggested, handing them up to Mikey.

"Excellent idea," Mikey told his friend.

Mikey positioned the blades around a giant string. Then he took one big chop, right above Fluffy's head.

This time Fluffy's furry face fell forward. With her sand-paper tongue, she licked Mikey right on the tip of his nose.

"Aw, geez," Mikey groaned, chopping away. "Don't kiss me, you stupid cat!"

In less than a minute, Fluffy was free. Unfortunately, Mikey had done so much chopping, there wasn't anything left of the web to show his mother. It was totally ruined. So was Fluffy's hair.

"Uh-oh," Mikey said as he climbed down the ladder with Fluffy. "Alison's gonna freak when she sees this!"

Mikey held the froufrou cat out for Max to see.

It was bad enough that Fluffy was covered with gooey bugs and sticky strings, but her long, fluffy hair wasn't so long anymore. At least not in six different places.

"You know she's gonna blame us when she sees Fluffy's hair," Mikey told Max.

"Don't worry," Max said. "We'll even it out so she won't notice. Then we'll give Fluffy a bath."

Mikey should have known that was a bad idea. Without thinking, he handed Max the hedge clippers.

By the time Max was done chopping, Fluffy looked more like a punk rocker than a froufrou cat.

Mikey buried his face in his hands.

"Maybe we can get Fluffy to run away from home," Max suggested.

Mikey nodded. It was the only solution.

Only Fluffy wouldn't go. Even after Mikey tossed her all the way down the street.

"We're dead," Mikey said as Fluffy darted right past them, heading for her cat door that led into the house.

"Yeah," Max agreed. "We're definitely dead."

There was nothing to do now but clean up the driveway. At least that way his mother wouldn't start screaming *before* she got out of the car.

The problem was, neither one of them wanted to touch a chicken carcass covered with poisonous spider spit.

But Max had a plan. "Get the hose," he ordered Mikey.

Mikey didn't want to ask. He just did as he was told.

Max's idea was to just spray all the gunk down the driveway into the street. Then they could squirt it into the sewer without touching a thing.

To Mikey's surprise, it was a good plan. As Mikey sprayed away, the garbage sailed toward the street. Until the water pressure died.

"Something's wrong with the hose," Mikey told Max, trying to get the water to squirt through the nozzle. "It's not spraying anymore."

"Maybe the hose got twisted up," Max said. "That happens to my father all the time."

Max headed back toward the house to check it out while Mikey stayed behind to untwist the spray nozzle from the end of the hose. *Maybe the stupid thing is stopped up,* he thought.

And boy, was it!

As Mikey yanked off the nozzle, hundreds of tiny white pearls dropped to the ground. But that was nothing compared with the number of pearly beads that suddenly shot out of the hose he was holding in his other hand. Spider eggs flew everywhere!

"Max!" Mikey screamed down the driveway. "Turn off the hose!"

But Max didn't hear him. Because Max was screaming in horror too.

CHAPTER 20

Mikey couldn't believe his eyes as he raced up the driveway toward Max. The other end of the hose was blown up so big, it looked like a beach ball was stuck inside it.

Only the big blob wasn't a ball. And it wasn't stuck either. In fact, it started rolling through the hose.

"What the heck is going on?" Max screamed as he watched the blob travel along the length of the hose.

"I don't know," Mikey cried back. "But spider eggs are shooting out of the other end like crazy!"

Max gulped. "Well, if that's a spider egg, we're in big trouble!"

Just then the end of the hose whipped around toward them, like a long, winding snake ready to attack. Within seconds, the squiggly green tube began firing away at them with the force of a machine gun!

Spider-filled BBs tore through the air. They hit so hard that Mikey was afraid they would tear through his clothes and rip through his body.

"Do something!" Max cried in a panic.

"Like what?" Mikey cried back.

They both froze as the blob in the hose started blowing up even bigger. Then it stopped moving.

The spider bullets stopped firing.

Mikey ran for the nozzle.

"What are you doing?" Max said.

"I'm going to screw the nozzle back on so that giant egg can't get out," he told Max.

"Good idea," Max agreed.

But just as Mikey started to twist on the nozzle, the blob in the hose started moving again. Only this time it wasn't rolling!

Mikey couldn't believe what he was seeing. The hose was stretching and bending as if someone was pushing against the inside of it.

"That's not a spider egg in there!" Mikey cried, dropping the nozzle. "That's a spider! A big killer spider!"

A giant, hairy leg shot out of the hose and wrapped itself around Mikey's throat. Mikey frantically managed to pull away, but the sharp claw on the end of the spider's leg ripped through his shirt and scratched the front of his chest.

A second hairy leg came shooting out, but before it could grab another piece of Mikey's flesh, Mikey started to run, with Max right behind him.

They raced for the garage. So did the hose.

It was slithering down the driveway like a giant green snake with two hairy legs sticking out of its head.

Mikey hit the switch on the wall to close the garage door the second they got inside.

"Hurry up and close, you stupid door!" Max cried.

Mikey stood watching the driveway, terrified.

The hose shot up the driveway as the garage door began to descend. The spider's legs sticking out of the top were peeling back the green rubber tube like the skin of a banana.

Suddenly eight bulging black eyeballs emerged— eyeballs the size of major league baseballs.

Mikey let out a scream that could have shattered every window in the house. He was sure that he and Max were about to end up like the chicken bones in the garbage.

The spider lunged forward, baring its giant, razor-sharp fangs.

Just in the nick of time, the garage door slammed shut, sealing Mikey and Max safely inside. But Mikey knew they wouldn't be safe for long.

The spider was disappearing back into the hose, working its way through the rubbery tube toward the faucet that led to the pipes in the house.

CHAPTER 21

"Maybe we should call a plumber," Max suggested later, as the two boys sat in Mikey's room.

"A plumber isn't going to do us any good," Mikey said. "What we need is an exterminator."

They certainly needed somebody to help them get rid of their spider problem. And it wasn't going to be Mikey's mom.

She didn't believe that there was a giant spider lurking in her pipes. In fact, she didn't believe that there were any spiders at all. She blamed everything that had happened on Mikey and Max. And she was more furious with them than ever after she saw Fluffy's haircut.

The two of them had been banished to Mikey's room once again.

"How much do you figure an exterminator costs?" Max asked.

"I don't know." Mikey shrugged. "How much do you have?"

Max emptied out his pockets and counted up what he had. "Three dollars and eighteen cents," he informed Mikey.

"We're going to need a lot more than that," Mikey said. He'd already emptied his own pockets and was working on his bank.

All told, they had less than ten dollars.

"We've got to get more money," Mikey said, pointing out the obvious.

"Yeah," Max agreed. "But where? Your mom's certainly not going to give it to us. She won't even talk to us."

There was only one place to go.

"Alison has a ton of baby-sitting money stashed away," Mikey said.

"She's not going to give any of it to us," Max assured him. "Not a chance."

But it was their only shot.

"Maybe if we promise to pay her back with interest," Mikey said as hopefully as he could. But he didn't believe it for a minute. Still, they had to try.

They found Alison with her face pressed up against the bathroom mirror, loading on makeup for her skating party. Alison was the only one who was getting to go to Ice Land. It was one more reason for Mikey to hate her.

"Hi, Alison," Mikey said, trying to sound nice.

"Get away from me," she snapped, not even looking at them.

"Listen, Alison. We've got big problems," Max said.

"You're telling me," Alison shot back. "Starting with your faces." She cracked herself up.

"Alison, please," Mikey begged. He was trying not to think about how humiliating it was to be nice to her, let alone ask her for something. "We need your help," he continued.

Alison kept working on her face. She never took her eyes off herself. "What do you want?" she asked.

"We need to borrow some money," Mikey explained.

Alison just laughed.

Mikey was trying to figure out what to say next when he saw something terrible. The lid on the toilet was slowly rising, all by itself. Something was in there trying to get out!

Mikey swallowed hard as a big, hairy spider leg shot out over the edge of the bowl.

"Alison!" Mikey gasped. He couldn't take his eyes off the monstrous leg that was reaching out of the toilet.

But Alison didn't see it. It was behind her and she was looking at Mikey.

"Forget it, you little dork," Alison sneered. "There's no way you're getting a penny from me."

"Alison, you don't understand," Mikey said, pointing behind her, trying to get her to turn around and look.

A second leg shot out of the toilet.

"Alison!" Mikey shrieked in a panic.

"Get lost!" Alison slammed the door right in Mikey's face and flipped the lock.

Mikey couldn't believe it. Once upon a time, it would have been a dream come true—Alison locked inside the bathroom with a giant killer spider!

But now he knew he had to do something. "We've got to help her," he told Max.

"How?" Max asked. "She won't listen to a word we say."

"Maybe we should break down the door," Mikey suggested. "We can't just leave her in there so that the spider can eat her!"

"Why not?" Max shot back. "It would serve her right. Besides, I'll bet that spider doesn't want to get anywhere near Alison either."

Mikey ignored Max. He pressed his ear up against the door. But he couldn't hear a thing.

"How come she's not screaming?" Max wanted to know.

That was what Mikey wanted to know too. He hoped that the giant spider hadn't eaten her already.

As Mikey continued to listen, an ear-piercing scream shook the door.

It was Alison. "Oh, no!" she shrieked. "Look at this thing! It's a monster!"

CHAPTER 22

The bathroom door flew open and Alison practically knocked both boys over as she pushed passed them.

"Alison, what happened in there?" Mikey asked.

Alison didn't answer. She just stormed down the hallway toward the stairs.

"Mommy!" Alison called as she started down. "I can't go to the party. I have a monster zit eating off my nose. I can't let anybody see me looking like this!"

On any other day, Mikey and Max would have teased Alison until she cried. But today was different. Today they had much more important things to think about—like a gigantic, flesh-eating spider.

Mikey peeked inside the bathroom.

But there was nothing to see. Everything seemed to be in order. There wasn't a sign of a killer spider anywhere.

Even the lid on the toilet seemed to be closed tight.

"Mikey!" A voice made him jump. "Max!" It was Mikey's mother. She was calling to them from the bottom of the stairs. "I'm taking Alison to her party now. I expect you to behave while I'm gone."

"Okay, Mom," Mikey called back. "We will."

Mikey's mom didn't wait for his answer. Mikey heard the front door close before he'd even finished talking.

Now he and Max were alone. But just for a second.

The lid of the toilet blew open like someone had set off a firecracker inside the bowl.

Water gushed to the ceiling before it started spraying out in all directions, just like the fountain in the center of the mall.

But water wasn't the only thing that came out of the toilet. One by one, the spider's eight legs began to appear.

"AaaAAAgggGGGhhhHHH!" Max started screaming like a siren. "We're going to die!" he cried with the last ounce of breath he had in his lungs. Then he sucked in some more air and started screaming again.

"Run!" Mikey shouted over Max's screams. "We have to get out of here."

Max stood frozen to the spot and kept right on screaming. The dangly thing at the back of his throat was moving like crazy, but his feet weren't budging an inch.

"Run!" Mikey screamed again as the spider's head came up. Its huge fangs snapped together as its eight eyeballs locked on Mikey and Max.

Mikey pushed Max to get him moving. But Max

tripped over his own feet and fell. Mikey toppled onto him.

The spider climbed out of the toilet and crept toward them.

Mikey scrambled to get to his feet. But Max kept pulling him down.

With one more step, the spider would be standing right over them. Its red-speckled body would clear their heads by a foot, and its eight hairy, huge legs would surround them like bars. Mikey and Max would be trapped in a bug cage until the spider decided to eat them.

CHAPTER 23

"I don't want to die!" Max cried as the spider loomed over them.

"Then run, you moron!" Mikey scrambled to his feet. He pulled Max up by the shirt collar. Together they took off, running for the stairs.

"Hurry up!" Max screamed, pushing Mikey down three steps at a time. "He's coming after us!"

Mikey was afraid to look back. But he did. The spider sat on the landing, looking over the balcony.

"He is not!" Mikey cried. "He's just watching us!" But Mikey was wrong.

Just as he and Max reached the foyer, the spider leaped over the railing. Mikey looked up in horror. The flesh-eating killer was about to land on top of them!

Mikey ran for the front door, but Max beat him to it. In

less than a millisecond, Max was out of the house and running. So was Mikey. And so was the spider.

Mikey couldn't believe how fast the spider could move. Its long legs propelled it forward so quickly and gracefully, it didn't look like it even touched the ground.

"What are we going to do?" Max gasped as they tore down the driveway.

"Just keep running!" Mikey screamed as they finally hit the street. "Maybe we can catch up with my mom!"

There wasn't another house around for miles, and the only other living creature in sight was a giant killer spider, who was starting to close in on them fast!

"Look!" Max screamed, pointing up ahead. "There's a car!"

The car was pretty far away, but Mikey could tell that it wasn't his mom's. He didn't care. For once, any adult was better than no adult at all.

"Hey, mister!" Mikey and Max shouted as they ran for their lives. "Help!"

But the car didn't even slow down as it disappeared around a curve. Mikey and Max were on their own.

Luckily, they'd been running so fast, they'd managed to get a pretty good lead on the spider.

Mikey needed it too, because his side felt ready to burst.

"I've got to stop for a second," he said, doubling over to rub the cramp in his side.

"Me too," Max agreed, panting up a storm.

To their surprise, the spider stopped too.

"Maybe *he's* got a cramp," Mikey said.

"I doubt it," Max shot back. "That sucker's got six more legs than we do. No way he's tired of running."

Max had a point.

"Maybe he's just giving up," Mikey suggested hopefully.

"Maybe." Max sounded pretty hopeful too.

"He must be," Mikey tried to convince himself. "I mean, why else would he stop?"

Just then Mikey got his answer. Only it wasn't from Max. It was from the spider. And Mikey didn't even see it coming.

A thick web string shot out of the spider and flew down the street. Before Mikey even had a chance to scream, he was roped and tied. The sticky, wet lasso wrapped itself around his ankles and pulled him to the ground.

The spider wasn't giving up at all, Mikey realized. It was coming in for the kill.

CHAPTER 24

"Help me!" Mikey screamed as the giant spider started dragging him back toward the house.

Max grabbed on to Mikey's hand and held tight.

But that didn't stop the spider. It kept pulling and pulling until Mikey felt as though he was going to be torn in two.

"Let go of my hand," Mikey screamed at Max. "Grab hold of the spider's string so I can get free."

As Max let go of Mikey's hand, Mikey was yanked forward. The spider's string contracted like a stretched-out rubber band being released. Mikey was moving so fast, he was afraid Max wouldn't be able to catch up.

"Hurry!" Mikey screamed.

Max was already running like crazy.

Every inch of Mikey's body was being bumped and

battered painfully along the gravel road. Mikey was sure he was going to end up one big black-and-blue mark. If he survived.

Max finally caught up. He reached out to grab the spider's string. He missed, and Mikey shot ahead again.

Max gave it another try. This time he dove for the shiny white rope with both hands.

"Oh, gross!" Max screamed the second he grabbed it. "This thing is really sticky!"

Max dug in his heels, trying to pull the spider to a stop. But it didn't work. The spider kept pulling them forward.

"Pull harder!" Mikey shouted frantically.

"I'm trying!" Max shouted back. He put all his weight into it, grunting and groaning in the struggle.

Mikey felt himself slowing down. Then he wasn't moving at all. Without wasting a single moment, he got himself into a sitting position and started working to get free.

But the spider's string was sticky and thick, and it was coiled around Mikey's ankles so tightly, he couldn't budge it.

"Hurry up!" Max shouted. "I can't hold him back forever."

He couldn't even hold him back another minute.

Mikey fell backward again as the spider jerked forward.

"We're never going to get you free like this!" Max cried. Then he took off running.

"Don't leave me!" Mikey called out in a panic.

"I'm not," Max hollered back, sounding just as panicked. "I'm going to get the hedge clippers so I can cut you loose."

Mikey couldn't believe that Max was thinking clearly enough to come up with such a great idea. It was the perfect solution. A couple of chops with the hedge clippers and Mikey would be free!

For a moment, Mikey started to calm down. But it was only for a moment.

As Mikey watched Max run toward the garage, he saw something horrifying.

"Max!" Mikey cried out to warn him.

Mikey shouldn't have done that. As Max turned toward the sound of Mikey's voice, he missed seeing that he was headed right into a death trap! Mikey could see it glinting in the sunlight.

"Max!" he called out again, pointing toward the garage door.

A giant spiderweb covered the opening.

"Look out!" Mikey screamed. But it was too late. Max slammed right into the death trap and stuck like a bug.

CHAPTER 25

Max was glued to the huge sticky web, just the way Fluffy had been. The only difference was that there was no one to chop him free.

The spider continued to drag Mikey over the gravel, but now it was changing direction and heading toward the garage, where Max was stuck in the web.

"Help me!" Max screamed. "Don't let him get me!"

Mikey's heart was racing. Desperately he kicked and jerked furiously, trying to break free. But all he managed to do was bruise himself more.

"Help!" Max kept screaming. "Somebody please help us!"

Mikey saw Max tugging against the web, but it was useless. He couldn't get out.

Neither could Mikey.

They were both about to become the spider's dinner.

It couldn't end like this—being devoured by a flesh-eating spider! Mikey started kicking even more wildly than before. He didn't feel the bumps and bruises anymore. He didn't feel anything but fear.

He didn't even feel that his foot had slipped out of his work boot. He was kicking and screaming so furiously, it took him several seconds to realize that one foot was free!

There was hope. But there wasn't much time. The spider was moving up the driveway fast.

Mikey used his free foot to try to push the boot off his other foot. It wasn't budging.

"Help! Help!" Max's cries became more frantic as the spider closed in on him.

Mikey kept working at the boot. If he didn't get it off soon, Max would be dead.

Mikey kicked as hard as he could. Suddenly the boot went flying. Mikey was free!

Unfortunately, the spider noticed. It stopped moving forward before Mikey could get to his feet, turned around, and glared at him.

Mikey scrambled backward in a panic. The spider lifted one of its long legs and stepped toward him.

Mikey let out a scream, sure that the spider was going to pounce.

But the spider took only one step forward, then turned around to look at Max. It was as if the spider was trying to decide which one of them to eat first.

If the spider went for Max, Max was a goner. At least Mikey had a fighting chance. Mikey knew what he had to do. He had to lure the spider away from Max.

As he got to his feet, Mikey grabbed a pebble from the driveway and threw it at the spider. It bounced right off its armorlike body. But the pebble did the trick. Just as Mikey had hoped, the spider turned around to face him.

"Come and get me, you hairy monster," Mikey taunted the spider.

The spider didn't make a move.

Mikey threw a whole handful of gravel. Then he ducked as the stones bounced off the spider's face, right back at him.

"What are you, chicken?" Mikey growled. "Come and get me!"

Mikey forced himself to stay put as the spider crept toward him. The spider took a second step, then a third.

Mikey's heart was beating against the inside of his rib cage as if it were trying to break out.

Run, his brain screamed at him. *Run!*

He wanted one more second. Then he obeyed. Mikey took off down the driveway, picking up speed with every step.

"Help! Help!" Max's screams made Mikey look back. The spider had psyched him out again. It wasn't following Mikey at all.

It was headed for Max, baring its razor-sharp fangs!

CHAPTER 26

"Stop him, Mikey!" Max screamed as the spider moved closer and closer.

Max was trying to pull out of his clothes so that he could escape from the spider's web. But there was no way he would be able to do it in time.

"Leave him alone!" Mikey hollered at the spider as he ran up the driveway throwing handfuls of gravel at the monster.

The spider ignored Mikey and kept moving toward Max.

"You've got to stop him!" Max shrieked.

"How?" Mikey cried.

"Blow on him or something!" Max suggested frantically.

That was about the dumbest idea Mikey had ever heard, but he tried it anyway. He ran up behind the spider, as close as he could get, and started blowing with everything he had.

"It's not working!" Max screamed. "Blow harder!"

Mikey couldn't blow any harder. He was already beginning to feel dizzy from the effort. It was hopeless. Even the big bad wolf couldn't huff and puff hard enough to stop this sucker.

But just as he was about to give up, Mikey found a way to blow harder.

The leaf blower was lying on the ground a few feet away, right where they'd left it.

Mikey lunged for it. He pulled on the cord to start up the engine.

"Come on!" Mikey snapped at the machine as it sputtered—and then stopped. Mikey pulled the cord again and again.

"Hurry!" Max urged him.

"I can't get this stupid thing to work," Mikey said as he kept pulling the cord.

"Help!" Max cried.

The spider was hovering over Max. Its mouth was open, its huge fangs dripping.

With one final pull, Mikey made the leaf blower roar to life.

Without a second to spare, Mikey aimed the nozzle right at the spider's face.

It worked. The spider stood as still as a statue.

"Now what?" Mikey shouted over the sound of the leaf blower.

"You've got to cut me down," Max told him.

"How?" Mikey asked. "I need both hands to hold on to the leaf blower. You're going to have to find a way to get free. And hurry. I can't stand here holding this thing all day." His arms were getting tired already.

Suddenly the engine on the leaf blower sputtered and died.

CHAPTER 27

Mikey started pulling on the cord frantically. But the leaf blower wouldn't start up again.

"It's out of gas!" Mikey cried in a panic.

But the giant killer spider wasn't. *It* started to growl.

"Uh-oh!" Max yelped, trying to wiggle out of his pants. "I think he's really, *really* mad at us now!"

Mad wasn't the word for it.

The spider was screaming furiously. And its foul-smelling breath was hitting Mikey right in the face.

Mikey started to gag.

But before he could even cover his nose, the spider did something else. It started to blow. Hot, stinky air rose like a tornado from its bug guts.

Mikey went sailing. He could actually see the spider's foul breath swirling around him as it lifted him off the ground and sent him flying across the front lawn.

"Mikey!" Max's screams barely cut through the horrible smelling wind that whirled around Mikey's body. "Grab hold of a tree or something!"

Mikey tried, but the stream of hot air was moving him so quickly that every tree on the lawn seemed to blow right past him.

Suddenly the spider ran out of air. Mikey fell to the ground hard. Before he even had a chance to look up, Max started screaming again.

"Mikey!" he cried in a panic. "Get up! Hurry!"

Mikey was terrified that the spider had turned its attention back to Max.

But the spider wasn't attacking Max. Instead, it was running across the lawn toward Mikey at full speed!

"Mikey!" Max kept yelling. "Get up!"

Mikey scrambled to his feet as the spider flew toward him.

"Run!" Max shouted.

Mikey did. But he'd taken only a couple of steps before he tripped. Mikey opened his mouth to scream. But then he realized what it was that he'd tripped over.

It was the gas can he and Max had left out on the lawn when they were blowing the leaves!

Mikey sprang up like a shot. But just as he grabbed the can, the spider leaped forward.

Mikey knew that there was no way he could run past the spider without being caught by it. There was only one thing he could do. And he was going to need all the courage he could muster.

"You'll never catch me, you big, smelly bug!" Mikey screamed in the spider's face. Then he turned around and started to run farther away from the garage.

The spider did exactly what Mikey hoped it would. It ran after him.

Please let this work! Mikey thought as the spider closed in on his back. The horrible creature was so close that Mikey could feel its wiry leg hairs pinching through his shirt.

Now! Mikey thought.

Mikey jerked to a sudden stop and ducked.

The spider kept running, its red-speckled body whizzing right over Mikey's head.

"Psych out!" Mikey shouted at the spider. Then he took off for the garage.

"Way to go!" Max congratulated Mikey on the maneuver.

"Thanks," Mikey said.

"Hurry and cut me down!" Max ordered. He was halfway out of his pants, but he was still stuck to the web like glue.

Unfortunately, Max was going to have to stay that way. The spider was on his way back!

"I have to start blowing," Mikey said as he unscrewed the lid on the gas can. "Otherwise we'll never have a chance."

"Get me the hedge clippers first!" Max cried.

"I can't!" Mikey said, pouring the gas into the leaf blower. "There isn't enough time!"

There wasn't either.

The spider was back on the driveway as Mikey pulled the cord. The leaf blower sputtered and spit before it finally started to blow.

Mikey let out a sigh of relief as he pointed the nozzle at the spider's eyes.

The spider stood frozen. But only for a second. And Mikey was almost sure he heard the spider scream "psych" before it lunged for him.

"Mikey! Look out!"

Max didn't have to scream for Mikey to see what was looming over his head—fangs! Dripping, drooling, flesh-eating fangs!

Mikey almost closed his eyes. He didn't want to watch the spider eat him. But then again, if the spider bit his head off, Mikey wouldn't see anything anyway.

Only Mikey didn't want to be headless. He didn't want to be a picked pile of bones in the driveway either.

But what was he going to do?

The spider opened its monstrous mouth and leaned over to chomp off Mikey's head!

Mikey had to do something fast.

"Take that, you giant bug ball!" Mikey cried as he crammed the leaf blower's nozzle into the spider's mouth.

The spider's fangs closed down around it as if it were Mikey's throat.

Mikey wondered what to do next. He didn't have to wonder for long.

The spider started to blow up like a balloon. Mikey

couldn't believe his eyes as the spider got bigger and bigger, like a balloon in a Thanksgiving Day parade.

"Keep blowing!" Max exclaimed. "Maybe it'll just fly away!"

That didn't happen. Something better did.

The spider exploded like fireworks!

Mikey and Max watched in delight as bug guts flew through the air.

CHAPTER 28

"Your mom still doesn't believe us," Max griped. He and Mikey were in the bathroom brushing their teeth. "We had a whole trash bag full of spider guts."

"Yeah," Mikey agreed. "But you shouldn't have put them on the couch!"

"How was I supposed to know the bag would break?" Max shot back.

Mikey shrugged. There was no point in arguing. At least they were alive—in big trouble, but alive.

"All I know is that I hate your sister!" Max said as he crammed his toothbrush into his mouth.

Mikey hated her more.

It was Alison's fault that they'd scooped up the spider guts in the first place. If Alison hadn't kept Mrs. Davis at the stupid skating party all night, their mother would have been home before it started to rain. And if she'd gotten home before it started to rain, she would have seen the spider guts in the driveway before they washed away. That was why Max had started scooping them up in the first place.

Mikey thought it was a good idea. How else could they prove to his mom that they'd risked life and limb fighting a giant, man-eating spider?

They'd managed to scoop up three shovelfuls before the rain sprayed the rest of the gooey, slimy, gloppy guts away.

Unfortunately, they'd also scooped up gravel and mud, which broke through the bag the second Max plopped it onto the couch.

The spider guts got smushed into gunk, Mikey's mother's couch got filthy, and Mikey and Max got sent straight to Mikey's room.

"Yeah," Mikey grumbled as he reached for his toothbrush. "I hate Alison too."

Mikey squeezed the toothpaste onto the brush and ran it under water before he stuck it into his mouth. "Move over," he ordered Max, shoving him with his elbow. "Give me some room."

"You've got room," Max huffed, shoving back.

"I do not," Mikey complained. "I can't even see in the mirror."

"Can't you brush your teeth without looking in the mirror?" Max said.

"No," Mikey answered. "I can't."

Mikey shoved again. Max finally moved.

Mikey looked in the mirror and started to brush.

Suddenly something caught his eye—and it wasn't his own reflection. Something was crawling across the glass, something dark and hairy, with long legs!

Mikey's heart started to pound. He was so scared, he almost swallowed his toothbrush. "Max!" he yelped. "There's another spider in here!"

"Where?" Max cried, practically jumping out of his pajamas.

Mikey pointed to the creature crawling across the glass.

Max started to laugh. "It's just a daddy longlegs, you idiot," Max pointed out.

Max was right. It was just a regular spider. "Oh, man." Mikey heaved a sigh of relief. "I almost had a heart attack."

"Over him?" Max cracked up even harder. "We just slaughtered the King Kong of killer spiders out there, and you're jumping over a daddy longlegs?"

Mikey started to laugh too.

"You want me to get the leaf blower?" Max kept on teasing.

"Very funny," Mikey said.

"Just grab him and flush him down the toilet," Max told him.

"Are you out of your mind?" Mikey shot back. "No way am I ever flushing another bug down the toilet. Who knows what'll happen when he gets into those pipes?"

"Cut me a break," Max said. "A-rack-knee-a-whatever-it-was was just a freak. I've flushed plenty of bugs before, and none of them ever turned into monsters."

"Oh, yeah?" Mikey challenged. "Then you do it."

"Fine," Max shot back. "I will."

But as Max reached for a tissue, the pipes in the sink started to gurgle. Mikey shot Max a worried look.

"It's just the water churning around," Max said. But his face started to turn pale—especially when the pipes began to croak!

"RI-BIT!"

The creepiest-sounding frog voice echoed through the bathroom.

"Uh-oh," Max cried, dropping the tissue fast. "It's that frog from the dissecting kit!"

"It can't be," Mikey yelped. "You cut him into smithereens!"

But it was. A long, slimy frog tongue shot out of the drain and grabbed the daddy longlegs on the mirror.

Mikey and Max were definitely in for some more plumbing problems.

Ready for more . . .

Here's a preview of the next spine-chilling book
from A. G. Cascone

GHOST KNIGHT

When Cody Adams visits his grandparents at Shady Acres Retirement Village, he doesn't expect to find much excitement. Then Cody meets Ben Cooper, the grounds-keeper's son, and the two boys set out on an adventure that will prove to be the knightmare of their lives. It all starts when Cody's cellular phone connects them to a ghost zone—and a deadly challenge from which there is no escape. In order for Cody and Ben to stay among the living, they have no choice but to enter the crumbling old castle that looms at the edge of the golf course . . . and face the spirits of the dead.

"Welcome, brave knights." The old ghost bowed to Cody and Ben.

Brave knights? What was this guy talking about?

"We're not brave knights!" Cody told him. He didn't really have to tell him that. It was pretty obvious. Ben was screaming his head off. And Cody was so scared, his knees were knocking together.

But the old man didn't seem to notice. Or maybe he just didn't care. Because he went right on talking as if Cody hadn't said anything at all.

"I am Lord Umberland," the ghost introduced himself. "I am the Protector of Her Royal Highness, the princess Gianna."

"Lord Umberland! You're the guy Jeevers said he was going to talk to," Cody exclaimed.

"Mr. Jeevers has a noble heart," Lord Umberland replied. "But he is somewhat befuddled, and well beyond his youth. While his company is most delightful," he went on, "he is no match for the unearthly presence that rules this castle."

What the heck is that supposed to mean? Cody wondered.

Ben was wondering the same thing. "Who the heck rules this castle?" Ben's quivering voice squeaked like a mouse.

"You will learn soon enough," Lord Umberland replied. "Come now," he told them. "Princess Gianna awaits you in the tower." He pulled the huge tapestry aside. "Take these stairs all the way to the top of the castle and you shall find her."

Jeevers wasn't the only one who was befuddled. Lord Umberland was out of his mind. There were no stairs behind the tapestry. Just a solid stone wall.

"Hurry," Lord Umberland urged them.

Neither Cody nor Ben made a move.

"There are no stairs," Cody finally pointed out.

"Of course there are," Lord Umberland insisted. "They're right here." He pointed.

Cody watched in amazement as a piece of the wall disappeared. Suddenly, a long, winding staircase stood before them.

"How did you do that?" Ben asked nervously.

"I did nothing," Lord Umberland answered.

"You just made stairs appear," Cody said.

"No." Lord Umberland smiled. "I did not. The stairs were always there. You just didn't see them until I pointed them out to you."

"How is that possible?" Cody asked.

"The more you believe, the more you will see," Lord Umberland answered. "Now you must go to my princess. There isn't much time."

"Time for what?" Cody asked as he moved slowly toward the stairs.

Lord Umberland didn't answer. All he said was "Please hurry."

Cody put his foot on the first step, testing to see if it was real. Hard stone met the bottom of his sneaker.

"Are you coming?" Cody asked, turning back to Ben.

Ben looked around the room, trying to find another way out. But there was none. "Do I have a choice?" he mumbled. Then he cautiously walked past Lord Umberland to follow Cody.

Cody glanced back to see if Lord Umberland was following them as well.

But Lord Umberland was gone. All that was left was the echo of his voice. "The stairs will take you where you need to go," he said.

Cody started climbing, with Ben close behind him.

The staircase was narrow and dimly lit. It went around in

a spiral, so Cody could see only a few feet in front of him. With every step he took, he feared something terrible might be lurking just around the corner.

He was so worried about what was in front of him, he never bothered to look behind.

Ben did.

"Uh, Cody . . ." Ben tugged on the back of Cody's shirt to get his attention. "You'd better hope there's another way down from here."

"What are you talking about?" Cody whirled around. Then he saw for himself. "Geez, oh, man," he cried. "What is going on?"

All the steps behind them had disappeared. There was nothing below but a gaping black hole.

Collect them all!

About the Author

A. G. Cascone is the pseudonym of two authors. Between them, they have written six previous books, two horror movie screenplays, and several pop songs, including one top-ten hit.

If you want to find out more about DEADTIME STORIES or A. G. Cascone, look on the World Wide Web at:
      http://www.bookwire.com/titles/deadtime/

Also, we'd love to hear from you! You can write to
      A. G. Cascone
      c/o Troll
      100 Corporate Drive
      Mahwah, NJ 07430-1404

Or you can send e-mail directly to:
      agcascone@bookwire.com